Being There

BOOKS BY JERZY KOSINSKI

NOVELS

The Painted Bird
Steps
Being There
The Devil Tree
Cockpit
Blind Date
Passion Play
Pinball
The Hermit of 69th Street

ESSAYS

Passing By
Notes of the Author
The Art of the Self

NONFICTION

(Under the pen name Joseph Novak)
The Future Is Ours, Comrade
No Third Path

Jerzy Kosinski

Being There

GROVE PRESS
New York

First published by Harcourt Brace Jovanovich, Inc.
Published simultaneously in Canada
Printed in the United States of America

Library of Congress Cataloging-in-Publication Data

Kosinski, Jerzy N., 1933–1991
        Being there / Jerzy Kosinski.
            p.   cm.
        ISBN 0-8021-3634-6
        I. Title.
    PS3561.O8B45   1999
    813'.54—dc21   99-10245

Grove Press
841 Broadway
New York, NY 10003

03   10 9 8 7

For Katherina v. F.
who taught me that love
is more than the longing
to be together

One

It was Sunday. Chance was in the garden. He moved slowly, dragging the green hose from one path to the next, carefully watching the flow of the water. Very gently he let the stream touch every plant, every flower, every branch of the garden. Plants were like people; they needed care to live, to survive their diseases, and to die peacefully.

Yet plants were different from people. No plant is able to think about itself or able to know itself; there is no mirror in which the plant can recognize its face; no plant can do anything intentionally: it cannot help growing, and its growth has no meaning, since a plant cannot reason or dream.

It was safe and secure in the garden, which was separated from the street by a high, red brick wall covered with ivy, and not even the sounds of the passing cars disturbed the peace. Chance ignored the streets. Though he had never stepped outside the house and its garden, he was not curious about life on the other side of the wall.

The front part of the house where the Old Man lived might just as well have been another part of the wall or the street. He could not tell if anything in it was alive or not. In the rear of the ground floor facing the garden, the maid lived. Across the hall Chance had his room and his bathroom and his corridor leading to the garden.

What was particularly nice about the garden was that, at any moment, standing in the narrow paths or amidst the bushes and trees, Chance could start to wander, never knowing whether he was going forward or backward, unsure whether he was ahead of or behind his previous steps. All that mattered was moving in his own time, like the growing plants.

Once in a while Chance would turn off the water and sit on the grass and think. The wind, mindless of direction, intermittently swayed the bushes and trees. The city's dust settled evenly, darkening the flowers, which waited patiently to be rinsed by the rain and dried by the sunshine. And yet, with all its life, even at the peak of its bloom, the garden was its own graveyard. Under every tree and bush lay rotten trunks and disintegrated and decomposing roots. It was hard to know which was more important: the garden's surface or the graveyard from which it grew and into which it was constantly lapsing. For example, there were some hedges at the wall which grew in complete disregard of the other plants; they grew faster, dwarfing the smaller flowers, and spreading onto the territory of weaker bushes.

Chance went inside and turned on the TV. The set created its own light, its own color, its own time. It did not follow the law of gravity that forever bent all plants downward. Everything on TV was tangled and mixed and yet smoothed out: night and day, big and small, tough and brittle, soft and rough, hot and cold, far and near. In this colored world of television, gardening was the white cane of a blind man.

By changing the channel he could change himself. He could go through phases, as garden plants went through phases, but he could change as rapidly as he wished by twisting the dial backward and forward. In some cases he could spread out into the screen without stopping, just as on TV people spread out into the screen. By turning the dial, Chance could bring others inside his eyelids. Thus he came to believe that it was he, Chance, and no one else, who made himself be.

The figure on the TV screen looked like his own reflection in a mirror. Though Chance could not read or write, he resembled the man on TV more than he differed from him. For example, their voices were alike.

He sank into the screen. Like sunlight and fresh air and mild rain, the world from outside the garden entered Chance, and Chance, like a TV image, floated into the world, buoyed up by a force he did not see and could not name.

He suddenly heard the creak of a window opening above his head and the voice of the fat maid calling. Reluctantly he got up, carefully turned off the TV, and stepped outside. The fat maid was leaning out of the upstairs window flapping her arms. He did not like her. She had come some time after black Louise had gotten sick and returned to Jamaica. She was fat. She was from abroad and spoke with a strange accent. She admitted that she did not understand the talk on the TV, which she watched in her room. As a rule he listened to her rapid speech only when she was bringing him food and telling him what the Old Man had eaten and what she thought he had said. Now she wanted him to come up quickly.

Chance began walking the three flights upstairs. He did not trust the elevator since the time black Louise had been trapped in it for hours. He walked down the long corridor until he reached the front of the house.

The last time he had seen this part of the house some of the trees in the garden, now tall and lofty, had been quite small and insignificant. There was no TV then. Catching sight of his reflection in the large hall mirror, Chance saw the image of himself as a small boy and then the image of the Old Man sitting in a huge chair. His hair was gray, his hands wrinkled and shriveled. The Old Man breathed heavily and had to pause frequently between words.

Chance walked through the rooms, which seemed empty; the heavily curtained windows barely admitted the daylight. Slowly he looked at the large pieces of furniture shrouded in old linen covers, and at the veiled mirrors. The words that the Old Man had spoken to him the first time had wormed their way into his memory like firm roots. Chance was an orphan, and it was the Old Man himself who had sheltered him in the house ever since Chance was a child. Chance's mother had died when he was born. No one, not even the Old Man, would tell him who his father was. While some could learn to read and write, Chance would never be able to manage this. Nor would he ever be able to understand much of what others were saying to him or around him. Chance was to work in the garden, where he would care for plants and grasses and trees which grew there peacefully. He would be as one of them: quiet, openhearted in the sunshine and heavy when it rained. His name was Chance because he had been born by chance. He had no family. Although his mother had been very pretty, her mind had been as damaged as his: the soft soil of his brain, the ground from which all his thoughts shot up, had been ruined forever. Therefore, he could not look for a place in the life led by people outside the house or the garden gate. Chance must limit his life to his quarters and to the garden; he must not enter other parts of the household or walk out into the street. His food would always be brought to his room by Louise, who would be the only person to see Chance and talk to him. No one else was allowed to enter Chance's room. Only the Old Man himself might walk and sit in the garden. Chance would do exactly what he was told or else he would be sent to a special home for the insane where, the Old Man said, he would be locked in a cell and forgotten.

Chance did what he was told. So did black Louise.

✳

As Chance gripped the handle of the heavy door, he heard the screeching voice of the maid. He entered and saw a room twice the height of all the others. Its walls were lined with built-in shelves, filled with books. On the large table flat leather folders were spread around.

The maid was shouting into the phone. She turned and, seeing him, pointed to the bed. Chance approached. The Old Man was propped against the stiff pillows and seemed poised intently, as if he were listening to a trickling whisper in the gutter. His shoulders sloped down at sharp angles, and his head, like a heavy fruit on a twig, hung down to one side. Chance stared into the Old Man's face. It was white, the upper jaw overlapped the lower lip of his mouth, and only one eye remained open, like the eye of a dead bird that sometimes lay in the garden. The maid put down the receiver, saying that she had just called the doctor, and he would come right away.

Chance gazed once more at the Old Man, mumbled good-bye, and walked out. He entered his room and turned on the TV.

Two

Later in the day, watching TV, Chance heard the sounds of a struggle coming from the upper floors of the house. He left his room and, hidden behind the large sculpture in the front hall, watched the men carry out the Old Man's body. With the Old Man gone, someone would have to decide what was going to happen to the house, to the new maid, and to himself. On TV, after people died, all kinds of changes took place—changes brought about by relatives, bank officials, lawyers, and businessmen.

But the day passed and no one came. Chance ate a simple dinner, watched a TV show and went to sleep.

*   *   *

He rose early as always, found the breakfast that had been left at his door by the maid, ate it, and went into the garden.

He checked the soil under the plants, inspected the flowers, snipped away dead leaves, and pruned the bushes. Everything was in order. It had rained during the night, and many fresh buds had emerged. He sat down and dozed in the sun.

As long as one didn't look at people, they did not exist. They began to exist, as on TV, when one turned one's eyes on them. Only then could they stay in one's mind before being erased by new images. The same was true of him. By looking at him, others could make him be clear, could open him up and unfold him; not to be seen was to blur and to fade out. Perhaps he was missing a lot by simply watching others on TV and not being watched by them. He was glad that now, after the Old Man had died, he was going to be seen by people he had never been seen by before.

When he heard the phone ring in his room, he rushed inside. A man's voice asked him to come to the study.

Chance quickly changed from working clothes into one of his best suits, carefully trimmed and combed his hair, put on a pair of large sunglasses, which he wore when working in the garden, and went upstairs. In the narrow, dim book-lined room, a man and a woman were looking at him. Both sat behind the large desk, where various papers were spread out before them. Chance remained in the center of the room, not knowing what to do. The man got up and took a few steps toward him, his hand outstretched.

"I am Thomas Franklin, of Hancock, Adams and Colby. We are the lawyers handling this estate. And this," he said, turning to the woman, "is my assistant, Miss Hayes." Chance shook the man's hand and looked at the woman. She smiled.

"The maid told me that a man has been living in the house, and works as the gardener." Franklin inclined his head toward Chance. "However, we have no record of a man—any man—either being employed by the deceased or residing in his house during any of the last forty years. May I ask you how many days you have been here?"

Chance was surprised that in so many papers spread on the desk his name was nowhere mentioned; it occurred to him that perhaps the garden was not mentioned there either. He hesitated. "I have lived in this house for as long as I can remember, ever since I was little, a long time before the Old Man broke his hip and began staying in bed most of the time. I was here before there were big bushes and before there were automatic sprinklers in the garden. Before television."

"You what?" Franklin asked. "You lived here—in this house—since you were a child? May I ask you what your name is?"

Chance was uneasy. He knew that a man's name had an important connection with his life. That was why people on TV always had two names—their own, outside of TV, and the one they adopted each time they performed. "My name is Chance," he said.

"Mr. Chance?" the lawyer asked.

Chance nodded.

"Let's look through our records," Mr. Franklin said. He picked up some of the papers heaped in front of him. "I have a complete record here of all those who were at any time employed by the deceased and by his estate. Although he was supposed to have a will, we were unable to find it. Indeed, the deceased left very few personal documents behind. However, we do have a list of all his employees," he emphasized, looking down at a document he held in his hand.

Chance waited.

"Please sit down, Mr. Chance," said the woman.

16

Chance pulled a chair toward the desk and sat down.

Mr. Franklin rested his head in his hand. "I am very puzzled, Mr. Chance," he said, without lifting his eyes from the paper he was studying, "but your name does not appear anywhere in our records. No one by the name of Chance has ever been connected with the deceased. Are you certain, Mr. Chance—truly certain—that you have indeed been employed in this house?"

Chance answered very deliberately: "I have always been the gardener here. I have worked in the garden in back of the house all my life. As long as I can remember. I was a little boy when I began. The trees were small, and there were practically no hedges. Look at the garden now."

Mr. Franklin quickly interrupted. "But there is not a single indication that a gardener has been living in this house and working here. We, that is—Miss Hayes and I—have been put in charge of the deceased's estate by our firm. We are in possession of all the inventories. I can assure you," he said, "that there is no account of your being employed. It is clear that at no time during the last forty years was a man employed in this house. Are you a professional gardener?"

"I am a gardener," said Chance. "No one knows the garden better than I. From the time I was a child, I am the only one who has ever worked here. There was someone else before me—a tall black man; he stayed only long enough to tell me what to do and show me how to do it; from that time, I have been on my own. I planted some of the trees," he said, his whole body pointing in the direction of the garden, "and the flowers, and I cleaned the paths and watered the plants. The Old Man himself used to come down to sit in the garden and read and rest there. But then he stopped."

Mr. Franklin walked from the window to the desk. "I would like to believe you, Mr. Chance," he said, "but, you see, if what you say is true, as you claim it to be, then—for some reason difficult to fathom—your presence in this house, your employment, hasn't been recorded in any of the existing documents. True," he murmured to his assistant, "there were very few people employed here; he retired from our firm at the age of seventy-two, more than twenty-five years ago, when his broken hip immobilized him. And yet," he said, "in spite of his advanced age, the deceased was always in control of his affairs, and those who were employed by him have always been properly listed with our firm—paid, insured, et cetera. We have a record, after Miss Louise left, of the employment of one 'imported' maid, and that's all."

"I know old Louise; she can tell you that I have lived and worked here. She was here ever since I can remember, ever since I was little. She brought my food to my room every day, and once in a while she would sit with me in the garden."

"Louise died, Mr. Chance," interrupted Franklin.

"She left for Jamaica," said Chance.

"Yes, but she fell ill and died recently," Miss Hayes explained.

"I did not know that she had died," said Chance quietly.

"Nevertheless," Mr. Franklin persisted, "anyone ever employed by the deceased has always been properly paid, and our firm has been in charge of all such matters; hence our complete record of the estate's affairs."

"I did not know any of the other people working in the house. I always stayed in my room and worked in the garden."

"I'd like to believe you. However, as far as your former existence in this house is concerned, there just isn't any trace of you. The new maid has no idea of how long you have been here. Our firm has been in possession of all the pertinent deeds, checks, insurance claims, for the last fifty years." He smiled. "At the time the deceased was a partner in the firm, some of us were not even born, or were very, very young." Miss Hayes laughed. Chance did not understand why she laughed.

Mr. Franklin returned to the documents. "During your employment and your residence here, Mr. Chance, can you recall signing any papers?"

"No, sir."

"Then in what manner were you paid?"

"I have never been given any money. I was given my meals, very good meals, and as much to eat as I wanted; I have my room with a bathroom and a window that looks out on the garden, and a new door was put in leading out into the garden. I was given a radio and then a television, a big color television set with remote control changer. It also has an alarm in it to wake me up in the morning."

"I know the kind you're referring to," said Mr. Franklin.

"I can go to the attic and choose any of the Old Man's suits. They all fit me very well. Look." Chance pointed to his suit. "I can also have his coats, and his shoes, even though they are a bit tight, and his shirts, though the collars are a bit small, and his ties and . . ."

"I understand," Mr. Franklin said.

"It's quite amazing how fashionable your clothes look," interjected Miss Hayes suddenly.

Chance smiled at her.

"It's astonishing how men's fashions of today have reverted to the styles of the twenties," she added.

"Well, well," Mr. Franklin said, attempting lightheartedness, "are you implying that my wardrobe is out of style?" He turned to Chance: "And so you haven't in any way been contracted for your work."

"I don't think I have."

"The deceased never promised you a salary or any other form of payment?" Mr. Franklin persisted.

"No. No one promised me anything. I hardly ever saw the Old Man. He did not come into the garden since the bushes on the left side were planted, and they're shoulder-high now. As a matter of fact, they were planted when there was no television yet, only radio. I remember listening to the radio while I was working in the garden and Louise coming downstairs and asking me to turn it down because the Old Man was asleep. He was already very old and sick."

Mr. Franklin almost jumped out of his chair. "Mr. Chance, I think it would simplify matters if you could produce some personal identification indicating your address. That would be a start. You know, a checkbook or driver's license or medical insurance card . . . you know."

"I don't have any of those things," said Chance.

"Just any card that states your name and address and your age."

Chance was silent.

"Perhaps your birth certificate?" Miss Hayes asked kindly.

"I don't have any papers."

"We shall need some proof of your having lived here," Mr. Franklin said firmly.

"But," said Chance, "you have me. I am here. What more proof do you need?"

"Have you ever been ill—that is, have you ever had to go to the hospital or to a doctor? Please understand," Mr. Franklin said tonelessly, "all we want is some evidence that you actually have been employed and resided here."

"I have never been ill," said Chance. "Never."

Mr. Franklin noticed the admiring look Miss Hayes gave the gardener. "I know," he said. "Tell me the name of your dentist."

"I have never gone to a dentist or to a doctor. I have never been outside of this house, and no one has ever been allowed to visit me. Louise went out sometimes, but I did not."

"I must be frank with you," Mr. Franklin said wearily. "There is no record of your having been here, of any wages paid to you, of any medical insurance." He stopped. "Have you paid any taxes?"

"No," said Chance.

"Have you served in the army?"

"No. I have seen the army on TV."

"Are you, by chance, related to the deceased?"

"No, I am not."

"Assuming that what you say is true," said Franklin flatly, "do you plan to make any claim against the estate of the deceased?"

Chance did not understand. "I am perfectly all right, sir," he said cautiously. "I'm fine. The garden is a good one. The sprinklers are only a few years old."

"Tell me," Miss Hayes interrupted, straightening up and throwing her head back, "what are your plans now? Are you going to work for someone else?"

Chance adjusted his sunglasses. He did not know what to say. Why would he have to leave the garden? "I would like to stay here and work in this garden," he said quietly.

Mr. Franklin shuffled the papers on the desk and drew out a page filled with fine print. "It's a simple formality," he said, handing the paper to Chance. "Would you be kind enough to read it now and—if you agree to it—to sign it where indicated?"

Chance picked up the paper. He held it in both hands and stared at it. He tried to calculate the time needed to read a page. On TV the time it took people to read legal papers varied. Chance knew that he should not reveal that he could not read or write. On TV programs people who did not know how to read or write were often mocked and ridiculed. He assumed a look of concentration, wrinkling his brow, scowling, now holding his chin between the thumb and the forefinger of his hand. "I can't sign it," he said returning the sheet to the lawyer. "I just can't."

"I see," Mr. Franklin said. "You mean therefore that you refuse to withdraw your claim?"

"I can't sign it, that's all," said Chance.

"As you wish," said Mr. Franklin. He gathered his documents together. "I must inform you, Mr. Chance," he said, "that this house will be closed tomorrow at noon. At that time, both doors and the gate to the garden will be locked. If, indeed, you do reside here, you will have to move out and take with you all your personal effects." He reached into his pocket and drew out a small calling card. "My name and the address and phone number of our firm are on this card."

Chance took the card and slipped it into the pocket of his vest. He knew that he had to leave the study now and go to his room. There was an afternoon TV program he always watched and did not want to miss. He got up, said good-bye, and left. On the staircase he threw the card away.

Three

Early Tuesday morning Chance carried a large heavy leather suitcase down from the attic, noting for the last time the portraits lining the walls. He packed, left his room, and then, his hand on the garden gate, thought suddenly of postponing his departure and returning to the garden, where he would be able to hide unseen for some time. He set the suitcase down and went back into the garden. All was peaceful there. The flowers stood slender and

27

erect. The electric water sprinkler spurted out a formless cloud of mist onto the shrubs. Chance felt with his fingers the prickly pine needles and the sprawling twigs of the hedge. They seemed to reach toward him.

For some time he stood in the garden looking around lazily in the morning sun. Then he disconnected the sprinkler and walked back to his room. He turned on the TV, sat down on the bed, and flicked the channel changer several times. Country houses, skyscrapers, newly built apartment houses, churches shot across the screen. He turned the set off. The image died; only a small blue dot hung in the center of the screen, as if forgotten by the rest of the world to which it belonged; then it too disappeared. The screen filled with grayness; it might have been a slab of stone.

Chance got up and now, on the way to the gate, he remembered to pick up the old key that for years had hung untouched on a board in the corridor next to his room. He walked to the gate and inserted the key; then, pulling the gate open, he crossed the threshold, abandoned the key in the lock, and closed the gate behind him. Now he could never return to the garden.

He was outside the gate. The sunlight dazzled his eyes. The sidewalks carried the passers-by away, the tops of the parked cars shimmered in the heat.

He was surprised: the street, the cars, the buildings, the people, the faint sounds were images already burned into his memory. So far, everything outside the gate resembled what he had seen on TV; if anything, objects and people were bigger, yet slower, simpler and more cumbersome. He had the feeling that he had seen it all.

He began to walk. In the middle of the block, he became conscious of the weight of his suitcase and of the heat: he was walking in the sun. He had found a narrow space between the cars parked against the curb and turned to leave the sidewalk, when suddenly he saw a car rapidly backing toward him. He attempted to leap out past the car's rear bumper, but the suitcase slowed him. He jumped, but too late. He was struck and jammed against the headlights of the stationary car behind him. Chance barely managed to raise one knee; he could not raise his other leg. He felt a piercing pain, and cried out, hammering against the trunk of the moving vehicle with his fist. The limousine stopped abruptly. Chance, his right leg raised above the bumper, his left one still trapped, could not move. The sweat drenched his body.

The chauffeur leaped from the limousine. He was black, in uniform, and carried his hat in his hand. He began to mumble words, then realized that Chance's leg was still pinned. Frightened, he ran back into the car and drove a few inches forward. Chance's calf was freed. He tried to stand on both feet, but collapsed onto the edge of the sidewalk. Instantly, the rear door of the car opened and a slender woman emerged. She bent over him. "I hope you're not badly hurt?"

Chance looked up at her. He had seen many women who looked like her on TV. "It's only my leg," he said, but his voice was trembling. "I think it was crushed a bit."

"Oh, dear God!" the woman said hoarsely. "Can you—would you please raise your trouser-leg so I can take a look?"

Chance pulled up his left trouser-leg. The middle of the calf was an already swelling red-bluish blotch.

"I hope nothing is broken," the woman said. "I can't tell you how sorry I am. My chauffeur has never had an accident before."

"It's all right," Chance said. "I feel somewhat better now."

"My husband has been very ill. We have his doctor and several nurses staying with us. The best thing, I think, would be to take you right home, unless, of course, you'd prefer to consult your own physician."

"I don't know what to do," said Chance.

"Do you mind seeing our doctor, then?"

"I don't mind at all," said Chance.

"Let's go," said the woman. "If the doctor advises it, we'll drive you straight to the hospital."

Chance leaned on the arm that the woman proffered him. Inside the limousine she sat next to him.

The chauffeur installed Chance's suitcase, and the limousine smoothly joined the morning traffic.

The woman introduced herself. "I am Mrs. Benjamin Rand. I am called EE by my friends, from my Christian names, Elizabeth Eve."

"EE," Chance repeated gravely.

"EE," said the lady, amused.

Chance recalled that in similar situations men on TV introduced themselves. "I am Chance," he stuttered and, when this didn't seem to be enough, added, "the gardener."

"Chauncey Gardiner," she repeated. Chance noticed that she had changed his name. He assumed that, as on TV, he must use his new name from now on. "My husband and I are very old friends of Basil and Perdita Gardiner," the woman continued. "Are you by any chance a relative of theirs, Mr. Gardiner?"

"No, I am not," Chance replied.

"Would you care for a little whisky or perhaps a little cognac?"

Chance was puzzled. The Old Man did not drink and had not permitted his servants to drink. But once in a while, black Louise had secretly drunk in the kitchen and, on her insistence a very few times, Chance had tasted alcohol.

"Thank you. Perhaps some cognac," he replied, suddenly feeling the pain in his leg.

"I see that you are suffering," said the woman.

She hastened to open a built-in bar in front of them, and from a silverish flask poured dark liquid into a monogrammed glass. "Please drink it all," she said. "It will do you good." Chance tasted the drink and sputtered. The woman smiled. "That's better. We'll be home soon and you'll be cared for. Just a little patience."

Chance sipped the drink. It was strong. He noticed a small TV set cleverly concealed above the bar. He was tempted to turn it on. He sipped his drink again as the car maneuvered slowly through the congested streets. "Does the TV work?" Chance asked.

"Yes. Of course it does."

"Can you—would you turn it on, please?"

"Certainly. It will take your mind off your pain." She leaned forward and pressed a button: images filled the screen. "Is there any particular channel, any program, that you want to watch?"

"No. This one is fine."

The small screen and the sounds of the TV separated them from the noise of the street. A car suddenly pulled in front of them, and the chauffeur braked sharply. As Chance braced himself for the sudden lurch, a pain pierced his leg. Everything spun around him; then his mind blanked, like a TV suddenly switched off.

He awoke in a room flooded with sunshine. EE was there. He lay on a very large bed.

"Mr. Gardiner," she was saying slowly. "You lost consciousness. But meanwhile we're home."

There was a knock at the door; it opened and a man appeared wearing a white smock and thick black-rimmed glasses and carrying a fat leather case. "I am your doctor," he said, "and you must be Mr. Gardiner, crushed and kidnaped by our charming hostess." Chance nodded. The doctor joked, "Your victim is very handsome. But now I'll have to examine him, and I'm sure you will prefer to leave us alone."

Before EE left, the doctor told her that Mr. Rand was asleep and should not be disturbed until late in the afternoon.

Chance's leg was tender; a purple bruise covered almost the entire calf.

"I'm afraid," said the doctor, "that I'll have to give you an injection so I can examine your leg without making you faint when I press it."

The doctor removed a syringe from his case. While he was filling it, Chance visualized all the TV incidents in which he had seen injections being given. He expected the injection to be painful, but he did not know how to show that he was afraid.

The doctor evidently noticed it. "Now, now," he said. "It's just a mild state of shock you're in, sir, and, though I doubt it, there may have been some damage to the bone." The injection was surprisingly quick, and Chance felt no pain.

After a few minutes the doctor reported that there had been no injury to the bone. "All you must do," he said, "is rest until this evening. Then if you feel like it, you can get up for dinner. Just make sure you don't put any weight on the injured leg. Meanwhile I'll instruct the nurse about your injections; you'll have one every three hours and a pill at mealtimes. If necessary, we'll arrange for X rays tomorrow. Now, have a good rest, sir." He left the room.

Chance was tired and sleepy. But when EE returned, he opened his eyes.

When one was addressed and viewed by others, one was safe. Whatever one did would then be interpreted by the others in the same way that one interpreted what they did. They could never know more about one than one knew about them.

"Mrs. Rand," he said. "I almost fell asleep."

"I am sorry if I disturbed you," she said. "But I've just been speaking to the doctor and he tells me that all you need is rest. Now, Mr. Gardiner—" She sat on a chair next to his bed. "I must tell you how very guilty I am and how responsible I feel for your accident. I do hope it will not inconvenience you too much."

"Please don't worry," Chance said. "I am very grateful for your help. I don't . . . I wouldn't . . ."

"It was the least we could do. Now is there anyone you would like to notify? Your wife? Your family?"

"I have no wife, no family."

"Perhaps your business associates? Please do feel free to use the telephone or send a cable or use our Telex. Would you like a secretary? My husband has been ill for so long that at present his staff has very little to do."

"No, thank you. There isn't anything I need."

"Surely there must be someone you would like to contact. . . . I hope you don't feel . . ."

"There is no one."

"Mr. Gardiner, if this is so—and please don't think that what I say is mere politeness—if you have no particular business to attend to right away, I would like you to stay here with us until your injury has completely healed. It would be dreadful for you to have to look after yourself in such a state. We've lots of room, and the best medical attention will be available to you. I hope you will not refuse."

Chance accepted the invitation. EE thanked him, and he then heard her order the servants to unpack his suitcase.

Chance woke up as a strip of light moved across his face from the opening in the heavy curtains. It was late in the afternoon. He felt dizzy; he was aware of the pain in his leg and uncertain of where he was. Then he recalled the accident, the car, the woman, and the doctor. Standing close to the bed, within reach of his hand, was a TV. He turned it on and gazed at the reassuring images. Then, just as he decided to get up and open the curtains, the phone rang. EE was calling him. She asked about his leg and wanted to know whether he was ready to have tea and sandwiches brought to him and whether she could come up and visit him now. He said yes.

A maid entered with a tray, which she set down on the bed. Slowly and carefully, Chance ate the delicate food, remembering such meals from TV.

He was resting against the pillows, watching television, when EE entered the room. As she pulled a chair closer to his bed, he reluctantly turned the set off. She wanted to know about his leg. He admitted to some pain. In his presence she telephoned the doctor, assuring him that the patient appeared to be feeling better.

She told Chance that Mr. Rand was much older than she; he was well into his seventies. Until his recent illness, her husband had been a vigorous man, and even now, in spite of his age and illness, he remained interested and active in his business. She regretted, she said, that they had no children of their own, particularly since Rand had broken off all relations with his former wife and with his grown son of that marriage. EE confessed that she felt responsible for the rupture between father and son, since Benjamin Rand had divorced the boy's mother to marry her.

Thinking that he ought to show a keen interest in what EE was saying, Chance resorted to repeating to her parts of her own sentences, a practice he had observed on TV. In this fashion he encouraged her to continue and elaborate. Each time Chance repeated EE's words, she brightened and looked more confident. In fact, she became so at ease that she began to punctuate her speech by touching, now his shoulder, now his arm. Her words seemed to float inside his head; he observed her as if she were on television. EE rested her weight back in the chair. A knock at the door interrupted her in mid-sentence.

It was the nurse with the injection. Before leaving, EE invited Chance to have dinner with her and Mr. Rand, who was beginning to feel better.

Chance wondered whether Mr. Rand would ask him to leave the house. The thought that he might have to leave did not upset him; he knew that eventually he would have to go but that, as on TV, what would follow next was hidden; he knew the actors on the new program were unknown. He did not have to be afraid, for everything that happened had its sequel, and the best that he could do was to wait patiently for his own forthcoming appearance.

Just as he was turning on the TV, a valet—a black man—came, carrying his clothes, which had been cleaned and pressed. The man's smile brought back the easy smile of old Louise.

* * *

EE called again, asking him to come down and join her and her husband for a drink before dinner. At the bottom of the stairs a servant escorted him to the drawing room, where EE and an elderly man were waiting. Chance noticed that EE's husband was old, almost as old as the Old Man. Chance took his hand, which was dry and hot; his handshake was weak. The man was looking at Chance's leg. "Don't put any strain on it," he said in a slow, clear voice. "How are you feeling? EE told me about your accident. A damned shame! No excuse for it!"

Chance hesitated a moment. "It's really nothing, sir. I feel quite well already. This is the first time in my life that I have had an accident."

A servant poured champagne. Chance had barely

begun to sip his when dinner was announced. The men followed EE to the dining room, where a table was laid for three. Chance noted the gleaming silver and the frosty sculptures in the corners of the room.

In deciding how to behave, Chance chose the TV program of a young businessman who often dined with his boss and the boss's daughter.

"You look like a healthy man, Mr. Gardiner," said Rand. "That's your good luck. But doesn't this accident prevent you from attending to your business?"

"As I have already told Mrs. Rand," Chance began slowly, "my house has been closed up, and I do not have any urgent business." He cut and ate his food carefully. "I was just expecting something to happen when I had the accident."

Mr. Rand removed his glasses, breathed onto the lenses, and polished them with his handkerchief. Then he settled the glasses back on and stared at Chance with expectation. Chance realized that his answer was not satisfactory. He looked up and saw EE's gaze.

"It is not easy, sir," he said, "to obtain a suitable place, a garden, in which one can work without interference and grow with the seasons. There can't be too many opportunities left any more. On TV . . ." he faltered. It dawned on him. "I've never seen a garden. I've seen forests and jungles and sometimes a tree or two. But a garden in which I can work and watch the things I've planted in it grow . . ." He felt sad.

Mr. Rand leaned across the table to him. "Very well put, Mr. Gardiner—I hope you don't mind if I call you Chauncey? A gardener! Isn't that the perfect description of what a real businessman is? A person who makes a flinty soil productive with the labor of his own hands, who waters it with the sweat of his own brow, and who creates a place of value for his family and for the community. Yes, Chauncey, what an excellent metaphor! A productive businessman is indeed a laborer in his own vineyard!"

The alacrity with which Mr. Rand responded relieved Chance; all was well. "Thank you sir," he murmured.

"Please . . . do call me Ben."

"Ben." Chance nodded. "The garden I left was such a place, and I know I won't ever find anything as wonderful. Everything which grew there was of my own doing: I planted seeds, I watered them, I watched them grow. But now it's all gone, and all that's left is the room upstairs." He pointed toward the ceiling.

Rand regarded him gently. "You're young, Chauncey; why do you have to talk about 'the room upstairs'? That's where I'm going soon, not you. You could almost be my son, you're so young. You and EE: both of you, so young."

"Ben, dear—" began EE.

"I know, I know," he interrupted, "you don't like

my bringing up our ages. But for me all that's left is a room upstairs."

Chance wondered what Rand meant by saying that he'd soon be in the room upstairs. How could he move in up there while he, Chance, was still in the house?

They ate in silence, Chance chewing slowly and ignoring the wine. On TV, wine put people in a state they could not control.

"Well," said Rand, "if you can't find a good opportunity soon, how will you take care of your family?"

"I have no family."

Rand's face clouded. "I don't understand it—a handsome, young man like you without a family? How can that be?"

"I've not had the time," said Chance.

Rand shook his head, impressed. "Your work was that demanding?"

"Ben, please—" EE broke in.

"I'm sure Chauncey doesn't mind answering my questions? Do you, Chauncey?"

Chance shook his head.

"Well . . . didn't you ever want a family?"

"I don't know what it is to have a family."

Rand murmured: "Then, indeed, you are alone, aren't you?"

After a silence, the servants brought in another course. Rand looked over at Chance.

"You know," he said, "there's something about you

that I like. I'm an old man, and I can speak to you frankly. You're direct: you grasp things quickly and you state them plainly. As you may be aware," Rand continued, "I am chairman of the board of the First American Financial Corporation. We have just begun a program to assist American businesses that have been harassed by inflation, excessive taxation, riots, and other indecencies. We want to offer the decent 'gardeners' of the business community a helping hand, so to speak. After all, they are our strongest defense against the conglomerates and the pollutants who so threaten our basic freedoms and the well-being of our middle class. We must discuss this at greater length; perhaps, when you are up and around, you can meet some of the other members of the board, who will acquaint you further with our projects and our goals."

Chance was glad that Rand immediately added: "I know, I know, you are not a man to act on the spur of the moment. But do think about what I've said, and remember that I'm very ill and don't know how much longer I'm going to be around. . . ."

EE began to protest, but Rand continued: "I am sick and weary with age. I feel like a tree whose roots have come to the surface. . . ."

Chance stopped listening. He missed his garden; in the Old Man's garden none of the trees ever had their roots surface or wither. There, all the trees were young and well cared for. In the silence he now felt widening around him, he said quickly: "I will consider what you've said. My leg still hurts, and it is difficult to decide."

"Good. Don't rush, Chauncey." Rand leaned over and patted Chance's shoulder. They rose and went into the library.

Four

On Wednesday, as Chance was dressing, the phone rang. He heard the voice of Rand: "Good morning, Chauncey. Mrs. Rand wanted me to wish you good morning for her too, since she won't be at home today. She had to fly to Denver. But there's another reason I called. The President will address the annual meeting of the Financial Institute today; he is flying to New York and has just telephoned me from his plane. He knows I am ill and that, as the chairman, I won't be able to preside over the meeting as scheduled. But as I am feeling somewhat better today, the President has graciously decided to visit me before the luncheon. It's nice of him, don't you think? Well, he's going to land at Kennedy and then come over to Manhattan by helicopter. We can expect him here in about an hour." He stopped; Chance could hear his labored breathing. "I want you to meet him, Chauncey. You'll enjoy it. The President is quite a man, quite a man, and I know that he'll like and appreciate you. Now listen: the Secret Service people will be here before long to look over the place. It's strictly routine, something they have to do, no matter what, no matter where. If you don't mind, my secretary will notify you when they arrive."

"All right, Benjamin, thank you."

"Oh, yes, one more thing, Chauncey. I hope you won't mind . . . but they will have to search you personally as well. Nowadays, no one in close proximity to the President is allowed to have any sharp objects on his person—so don't show them your mind, Chauncey, they may take it away from you! See you soon, my friend!" He hung up.

There must be no sharp objects. Chance quickly removed his tie clip and put his comb on the table. But what had Rand meant when he said "your mind"? Chance looked at himself in the mirror. He liked what he saw: his hair glistened, his skin was ruddy, his freshly pressed dark suit fitted his body as bark covers a tree. Pleased, he turned on the TV.

After a while, Rand's secretary called to say that the President's men were ready to come up. Four men entered the room, talking and smiling easily, and began to go through it with an assortment of complicated instruments.

Chance sat at the desk, watching TV. Changing channels, he suddenly saw a huge helicopter descending in a field in Central Park. The announcer explained that at that very moment the President of the United States was landing in the heart of New York City.

The Secret Service men stopped working to watch too. "Well, the Boss has arrived," one of them said. "We better hurry with the other rooms." Chance was alone when Rand's secretary called to announce the President's imminent arrival.

"Thank you," he said. "I guess I'd better go down right now, don't you think?" He stammered a bit.

"I think it is time, sir."

Chance walked downstairs. The Secret Service men were quietly moving around the corridors, the front hall and the elevator entrance. Some stood near the windows of the study; others were in the dining room, the living room, and in front of the library. Chance was searched by an agent, who quickly apologized and then opened the door to the library for him.

Rand approached and patted Chance's shoulder. "I'm so glad that you'll have the opportunity to meet the Chief Executive. He's a fine man, with a sense of justice nicely contained by the law and an excellent judgment of both the pulse and purse of the electorate. I must say, it's very thoughtful of him to come to visit me now. Don't you agree?"

Chance agreed.

"What a pity EE isn't here," Rand declared. "She's a great fan of the President and finds him very attractive. She telephoned from Denver, you know."

Chance said that he knew about EE's call.

"And you didn't talk to her? Well, she'll call again; she'll want to know your impressions of the President and of how things went. . . . If I should be asleep, Chauncey, you will speak to her, won't you, and tell her all about the meeting?"

"I'll be glad to. I hope you're feeling well, sir. You do look better."

Rand moved uneasily in his chair. "It's all make-up, Chauncey—all make-up. The nurse was here all night and through the morning, and I asked her to fix me up so the President won't feel I'm going to die during our talk. No one likes a dying man, Chauncey, because few know what death is. All we know is the terror of it. You're an exception, Chauncey, I can tell. I know that you're not afraid. That's what EE and I admire in you: your marvelous balance. You don't stagger back and forth between fear and hope; you're a truly peaceful man! Don't disagree; I'm old enough to be your father. I've lived a lot, trembled a lot, was surrounded by little men who forgot that we enter naked and exit naked and that no accountant can audit life in our favor."

Rand looked pallid. He reached for a pill, swallowed it, and sipped some water from a glass. A phone rang. He picked up the receiver and said briskly: "Mr. Gardiner and I are ready. Show the President into the library." He replaced the receiver and then removed the glass of water from the desk top, placing it behind him on a bookshelf. "The President is here, Chauncey. He's on the way."

Chance remembered seeing the President on a recent television program. In the sunshine of a cloudless day, a military parade had been in progress. The President stood on a raised platform, surrounded by military men in uniforms covered with glittering medals, and by civilians in dark glasses. Below, in the open field, never-ending columns of soldiers marched, their faces riveted upon their leader, who waved his hand. The President's eyes were veiled with distant thought.

He watched the thousands in their ranks, who were reduced by the TV screen to mere mounds of lifeless leaves swept forward by a driving wind. Suddenly, down from the skies, jets swooped in tight, faultless formations. The military observers and the civilians on the reviewing stand barely had time to raise their heads when, like bolts of lightning, the planes streaked past the President, hurling down thunderous booms. The President's head once more pervaded the screen. He gazed up at the disappearing planes; a fleeting smile softened his face.

*   *   *

"It's good to see you, Mr. President," Rand said, rising from his chair to greet a man of medium height who entered the room smiling. "How thoughtful of you to come all this way to look in on a dying man."

The President embraced him and led him to a chair. "Nonsense, Benjamin. Do sit down, now, and let me see you." The President seated himself on a sofa and turned to Chance.

"Mr. President," Rand said, "I want to introduce my dear friend, Mr. Chauncey Gardiner. Mr. Gardiner —the President of the United States of America." Rand sank into a chair, while the President extended his hand, a wide smile on his face. Remembering that during his TV press conferences, the President always looked straight at the viewers, Chance stared directly into the President's eyes.

"I'm delighted to meet you, Mr. Gardiner," the President said, leaning back on a sofa. "I've heard so much about you."

Chance wondered how the President could have heard anything about him. "Please do sit down, Mr. Gardiner," the President said. "Together, let's reprimand our friend Benjamin for the way he shuts himself up at home. Ben . . ." he leaned toward the old man—"this country needs you, and I, as your Chief Executive, haven't authorized you to retire."

"I am ready for oblivion, Mr. President," said Rand mildly, "and, what's more, I'm not complaining; the world parts with Rand, and Rand parts with the world: a fair trade, don't you agree? Security, tranquillity, a well-deserved rest: all the aims I have pursued will soon be realized."

"Now be serious, Ben!" The President waved his hand. "I have known you to be a philosopher, but above all you're a strong, active businessman! Let's talk about life!" He paused to light a cigarette. "What's this I hear about your not addressing the meeting of the Financial Institute today?"

"I can't, Mr. President," said Rand. "Doctor's orders. And what's more," he added, "I obey pain."

"Well . . . yes . . . after all, it's just another meeting. And even if you're not there in person, you'll be there in spirit. The Institute remains your creation; your life's stamp is on all its proceedings."

The men began a long conversation. Chance understood almost nothing of what they were saying, even though they often looked in his direction, as if to invite his participation. Chance thought that they purposely spoke in another language for reasons of secrecy, when suddenly the President addressed him: "And you, Mr. Gardiner? What do you think about the bad season on The Street?"

Chance shrank. He felt that the roots of his thoughts had been suddenly yanked out of their wet earth and thrust, tangled, into the unfriendly air. He stared at the carpet. Finally, he spoke: "In a garden," he said, "growth has its season. There are spring and summer, but there are also fall and winter. And then spring and summer again. As long as the roots are not severed, all is well and all will be well." He raised his eyes. Rand was looking at him, nodding. The President seemed quite pleased.

"I must admit, Mr. Gardiner," the President said, "that what you've just said is one of the most refreshing and optimistic statements I've heard in a very, very long time." He rose and stood erect, with his back to the fireplace. "Many of us forget that nature and society are one! Yes, though we have tried to cut ourselves off from nature, we are still part of it. Like nature, our economic system remains, in the long run, stable and rational, and that's why we must not fear to be at its mercy." The President hesitated for a moment, then turned to Rand. "We welcome the inevitable seasons of nature, yet we are upset by the seasons of our economy! How foolish of us!" He smiled at Chance. "I envy Mr. Gardiner his good solid sense. This is just what we lack on Capitol Hill." The President glanced at his watch, then lifted a hand to prevent Rand from rising. "No, no, Ben—you rest. I do hope to see you again soon. When you're feeling better, you and EE must come to visit us in Washington. And you, Mr. Gardiner . . . You will also honor me and my family with a visit, won't you? We'll all look forward to that!" He embraced Rand, shook hands swiftly with Chance, and strode out the door.

Rand hastily retrieved his glass of water, gulped down another pill, and slumped in his chair. "He is a decent fellow, the President, isn't he?" he asked Chance.

"Yes," said Chance, "though he looks taller on television."

"Oh, he certainly does!" Rand exclaimed. "But remember that he is a political being, who diplomatically waters with kindness every plant on his way, no matter what he really thinks. I do like him! By the way, Chauncey, did you agree with my position on credit and tight money as I presented it to the President?"

"I'm not sure I understood it. That's why I kept quiet."

"You said a lot, my dear Chauncey, quite a lot, and it is what you said and how you said it that pleased the President so much. He hears my sort of analysis from everyone, but, yours, unfortunately . . . seldom if ever at all."

The phone rang. Rand answered it and then informed Chance that the President and the Secret Service men had departed and that the nurse was waiting with an injection. He embraced Chance and excused himself. Chance went upstairs. When he turned the TV on, he saw the presidential motorcade moving along Fifth Avenue. Small crowds gathered on the sidewalks; the President's hand waved from the limousine's window. Chance did not know if he had actually shaken that hand only moments before.

*　*　*

The annual meeting of the Financial Institute opened in an atmosphere of expectation and high tension, following the disclosure that morning of the rise in national unemployment to an unprecedented level. Administration officials were reluctant to divulge what measures the President would propose to combat further stagnation of the economy. All of the public news media were on the alert.

In his speech the President reassured the public that no drastic governmental measures were forthcoming, even though there had been another sudden decline in productivity. "There was a time for spring," he said, "and a time for summer; but, unfortunately, as in a garden of the earth, there is also a time for the inevitable chill and storm of autumn and winter." The President stressed that as long as the seeds of industry remained firmly embedded in the life of the country, the economy was certain to flourish again.

In the short, informal question-and-answer period, the President revealed that he had "conducted multiple-level consultations" with members of the "Cabinet, House, and Senate, and also with prominent leaders of the business community." Here he paid tribute to Benjamin Turnbull Rand, chairman of the Institute, absent because of illness; he added that at Mr. Rand's home he had engaged in a most fruitful discussion with Rand and with Mr. Chauncey Gardiner on the beneficial effects of inflation. "Inflation would prune the dead limbs of savings, thus enlivening the vigorous trunk of industry." It was in the context of the President's speech that Chance's name first came to the attention of the news media.

✳   ✳   ✳

In the afternoon Rand's secretary said to Chance: "I have Mr. Tom Courtney of the New York *Times* on the line. Could you talk to him, sir, just for a few minutes? I think he wants to get some facts about you."

"I'll talk to him," said Chance.

The secretary put Courtney on. "I'm sorry to disturb you, Mr. Gardiner; I wouldn't have if I hadn't first talked to Mr. Rand." He paused for effect.

"Mr. Rand is a very sick man," said Chance.

"Well, yes . . . Anyway, he mentioned that because of your character and your vision there is a possibility of your joining the board of the First American Financial Corporation. Do you wish to comment on this?"

"No," said Chance. "Not now."

Another pause. "Since the New York *Times* is covering the President's speech and his visit to New York, we would like to be as exact as possible. Would you care to comment on the nature of the discussion that took place between you, Mr. Rand, and the President?"

"I enjoyed it very much."

"Good, sir. And so, it seems, did the President. But Mr. Gardiner," Courtney went on, with feigned casualness, "we at the *Times* would like very much to update our information on you, if you see what I mean. . . ." He laughed nervously. "To start with, what, for example, is the relationship between your business and that of the First American Financial Corporation?"

"I think you ought to ask Mr. Rand that," said Chance.

"Yes, of course. But since he is ill, I am taking the liberty of asking you."

Chance was silent. Courtney waited for an answer.

"I have nothing more to say," said Chance and hung up.

Courtney leaned back in his chair, frowning. It was getting late. He called his staff, and when they had come in he assumed his old casual manner. "All right, gentlemen. Let's start with the President's visit and speech. I talked to Rand. Chauncey Gardiner, the man mentioned by the President, is a businessman, it seems, a financier, and, according to Rand, a strong candidate for one of the vacant seats on the board of the First American Financial Corporation." He looked at his staffers, who expected to hear more.

"I also talked to Gardiner. Well . . ." Courtney paused. "He's very laconic and matter-of-fact. Anyway, we won't have enough time to round up all the information on Gardiner, so let's play up his prospective affiliation with Rand, his joining the board of the First American Financial, his advice to the President, and so forth."

*   *   *

Chance watched TV in his room. The President's speech at the luncheon of the Financial Institute was telecast on several channels; the few remaining programs showed only family games and children's adventures. Chance ate lunch in his room, continued to watch TV, and was just about to fall asleep when Rand's secretary called.

"The executives of the THIS EVENING television program have just phoned," she said excitedly, "and they want you to appear on the show tonight. They apologized for giving you such short notice, but they've only just now heard that the Vice President will be unable to appear on the show to discuss the President's speech. Because Mr. Rand is so ill, he will, of course, also be unable to appear, but he has suggested that you—a financier who has made so favorable an impression on the President—might be willing to come instead."

Chance could not imagine what being on TV involved. He wanted to see himself reduced to the size of the screen; he wanted to become an image, to dwell inside the set.

The secretary waited on the phone.

"It's all right with me," said Chance. "What do I have to do?"

"You don't have to do anything, sir," she said cheerfully. "The producer himself will pick you up in time for the show. It's a live program, so you have to be there half an hour before it goes on. You'll be THIS EVENING's main attraction tonight. I'll call them right back; they'll be delighted with your acceptance."

Chance turned on the TV. He wondered whether a person changed before or after appearing on the screen. Would he be changed forever or only during the time of his appearance? What part of himself would he leave behind when he finished the program? Would there be two Chances after the show: one Chance who watched TV and another who appeared on it?

Early that evening, Chance was visited by the producer of THIS EVENING—a short man in a dark suit. The producer explained that the President's speech had heightened interest in the nation's economic situation. ". . . and since the Vice President won't be able to appear on our show tonight," he continued, "we would be very grateful to have you tell our viewers exactly what is going on in the country's economy.

Occupying, as you do, a position of such intimacy with the President, you are a man ideally suited to provide the country with an explanation. On the show you can be as direct as you'd like to be. The host won't interrupt you at all while you're talking, but if he wants to break in he'll let you know by raising his left forefinger to his left eyebrow. This will mean that he wants either to ask you a new question or to emphasize what you've already said."

"I understand," said Chance.

"Well, if you're ready, sir, we can go; our makeup man will have to do only a minor touch-up." He smiled. "Our host, by the way, would be honored to meet you before the show goes on."

In the large limousine sent by the network, there were two small TV sets. As they drove along Park Avenue, Chance asked if a set could be turned on. He and the producer watched the program in silence.

The interior of the studio looked like all the TV studios Chance had ever seen on TV. He was escorted quickly to a large adjoining office and offered a drink, which he refused; instead, he had a cup of coffee. The host of the show appeared. Chance recognized him instantly; he had seen him many times on THIS EVENING, although he did not like talk shows very much.

While the host talked on and on to him, Chance

wondered what was going to happen next and when he would actually be televised. The host grew quiet at last, and the producer returned promptly with a make-up man. Chance sat in front of a mirror as the man covered his face with a thin layer of brownish powder. "Have you appeared on television a lot?" asked the make-up man.

"No," said Chance, "but I watch it all the time."

The make-up man and the producer chuckled politely. "Ready," said the make-up man, nodding and closing his case. "Good luck, sir." He turned and left.

Chance waited in an adjacent room. In one corner stood a large, bulky TV set. He saw the host appear and introduce the show. The audience applauded; the host laughed. The big, sharp-nosed cameras rolled smoothly around the stage. There was music, and the band leader flashed on screen, grinning.

Chance was astonished that television could portray itself; cameras watched themselves and, as they watched, they televised a program. This self-portrait was telecast on TV screens facing the stage and watched by the studio audience. Of all the manifold things there were in all the world—trees, grass, flowers, telephones, radios, elevators—only TV constantly held up a mirror to its own neither solid nor fluid face.

Suddenly the producer appeared and signaled Chance to follow him. They walked through the door and on past a heavy curtain. Chance heard the host pronounce his name. Then, as the producer stepped away, he found himself in the glare of the lights. He saw the audience in front of him; unlike the audiences he had seen on his own TV set, he could not distinguish individual faces in the crowd. Three large cameras stood on the small, square stage; on the right, the host sat at a leather-padded table. He beamed at Chance, rose with dignity, and introduced him; the audience applauded loudly. Imitating what he had so often seen on TV, Chance moved toward the vacant chair at the table. He sat down, and so did the host. The cameramen wheeled the cameras silently around them. The host leaned across the table toward Chance.

Facing the cameras and the audience, now barely visible in the background of the studio, Chance abandoned himself to what would happen. He was drained of thought, engaged, yet removed. The cameras were licking up the image of his body, were recording his every movement and noiselessly hurling them into millions of TV screens scattered throughout the world—into rooms, cars, boats, planes, living rooms, and bedrooms. He would be seen by more people than he could ever meet in his entire life—people who would never meet him. The people who watched him on their sets did not know who actually faced them; how could they, if they had never met him? Television reflected only people's surfaces; it also kept peeling their images from their bodies until they were sucked into the caverns of their viewers' eyes, forever beyond retrieval, to disappear. Facing the cameras with their unsensing triple lenses pointed at him like snouts, Chance became only an image for millions of real people. They would never know how real he was, since his thinking could not be televised. And to him, the viewers existed only as projections of his own thought, as images. He would never know how real they were, since he had never met them and did not know what they thought.

Chance heard the host say: "We here in the studio are very honored to have you with us tonight, Mr. Chauncey Gardiner, and so, I'm sure, are the more than forty million Americans who watch THIS EVENING nightly. We are especially grateful to you for filling in on such short notice for the Vice President, who was unfortunately prevented by pressing business from being with us tonight." The host paused for a second; there was complete silence in the studio. "I will be frank, Mr. Gardiner. Do you agree with the President's view of our economy?"

"Which view?" asked Chance.

The host smiled knowingly. "The view which the President set forth this afternoon in his major address to the Financial Institute of America. Before his speech, the President consulted with you, among his other financial advisers. . . ."

"Yes . . . ?" said Chance.

"What I mean is . . ." The host hesitated and glanced at his notes. "Well . . . let me give you an example: the President compared the economy of this country to a garden, and indicated that after a period of decline a time of growth would naturally follow. . . ."

"I know the garden very well," said Chance firmly. "I have worked in it all of my life. It's a good garden and a healthy one; its trees are healthy and so are its shrubs and flowers, as long as they are trimmed and watered in the right seasons. The garden needs a lot of care. I do agree with the President: everything in it will grow strong in due course. And there is still plenty of room in it for new trees and new flowers of all kinds."

Part of the audience interrupted to applaud and part booed. Looking at the TV set that stood to his right, Chance saw first his own face fill the screen. Then some faces in the audience were shown—they evidently approved his words; others appeared angry. The host's face returned to the screen, and Chance turned away from the set and faced him.

"Well, Mr. Gardiner," the host said, "that was very

well put indeed, and I think it was a booster for all of us who do not like to wallow in complaints or take delight in gloomy predictions! Let us be clear, Mr. Gardiner. It is your view, then, that the slowing of the economy, the downtrend in the stock market, the increase in unemployment . . . you believe that all of this is just another phase, another season, so to speak, in the growth of a garden. . . ."

"In a garden, things grow . . . but first, they must wither; trees have to lose their leaves in order to put forth new leaves, and to grow thicker and stronger and taller. Some trees die, but fresh saplings replace them. Gardens need a lot of care. But if you love your garden, you don't mind working in it, and waiting. Then in the proper season you will surely see it flourish."

Chance's last words were partly lost in the excited murmuring of the audience. Behind him, members of the band tapped their instruments; a few cried out loud bravos. Chance turned to the set beside him and saw his own face with the eyes turned to one side. The host lifted his hand to silence the audience, but the applause continued, punctuated by isolated boos. He rose slowly and motioned Chance to join him at center stage, where he embraced him ceremoniously. The applause mounted to uproar. Chance stood uncertainly. As the noise subsided, the host took Chance's hand and said: "Thank you, thank you, Mr. Gardiner. Yours is the spirit which this country so greatly needs. Let's hope it will help usher spring into our economy. Thank you again, Mr. Chauncey Gardiner —financier, presidential adviser, and true statesman!"

He escorted Chance back to the curtain, where the producer gently took him in hand. "You were great, sir, just great!" the producer exclaimed. "I've been producing this show for almost three years and I can't remember anything like it! I can tell you that the boss really loved it. It was great, really great!" He led Chance to the rear of the studio. Several employees waved to him warmly, while others turned away.

*   *   *

After dining with his wife and children, Thomas Franklin went into the den to work. There was simply not enough time for him to finish his work in the office, especially as Miss Hayes, his assistant, was on vacation.

He worked until he could no longer concentrate, then went to the bedroom. His wife was already in bed, watching a TV program of commentary on the President's speech. Franklin glanced at the set as he undressed. In the last two years, Franklin's stock market holdings had fallen to one third of their value, his savings were gone, and his share in the profits of his firm had recently diminished. He was not encouraged by the President's speech and hoped that the Vice President or, in his absence, this fellow Gardiner, might brighten his gloomy predicament. He threw off his trousers clumsily, neglecting to hang them in the automatic trouser-press which his wife had given him on his birthday, and sat down on the bed to watch THIS EVENING, which was just starting.

The host introduced Chauncey Gardiner. The guest moved forward. The image was sharp and the color faithful. But even before that full face materialized clearly on the screen, Franklin felt he had seen this man before somewhere. Had it been on TV, during one of the in-depth interviews through which the restless cameras showed every angle of a man's head and body? Perhaps he had even met Gardiner in person? There was something familiar about him, especially the way he was dressed.

He was so absorbed in trying to remember if and when he had actually met the man that he did not hear at all what Gardiner said and what it was exactly that had prompted the loudly applauding audience.

"What was that he said, dear?" he asked his wife.

"Wow!" she said, "how did you miss it? He just said that the economy is doing fine! The economy is supposed to be something like a garden: you know, things grow and things wilt. Gardiner thinks things will be okay!" She sat in bed looking at Franklin ruefully. "I told you that there was no need to give up our option on that place in Vermont or to put off the cruise. It's just like you—you're always the first one to panic! Ha! I told you so! It's only a mild frost —in the garden!"

Franklin once again stared distractedly at the screen. When and where the devil had he seen this fellow before?

"This Gardiner has quite a personality," his wife mused. "Manly; well-groomed; beautiful voice; sort of a cross between Ted Kennedy and Cary Grant. He's not one of those phony idealists, or IBM-ized technocrats."

Franklin reached for a sleeping pill. It was late and he was tired. Perhaps becoming a lawyer had been a mistake. Business . . . finance . . . Wall Street; they were probably better. But at forty he was too old to start taking chances. He envied Gardiner his looks, his success, his self-assurance. "Like a garden." He sighed audibly. Sure. If one could only believe that.

✳   ✳   ✳

On his way home from the studio, alone in the limousine, watching TV, Chance saw the host with his next guest, a voluptuous actress clad in an almost transparent gown. He heard his name mentioned by both the host and his guest; the actress smiled often and said that she found Chance good-looking and very masculine.

At Rand's house, one of the servants rushed out to open the door for him.

"That was a very fine speech you made, Mr. Gardiner." He trailed Chance to the elevator.

Another servant opened the elevator door. "Thank you, Mr. Gardiner," he said. "Just 'thank you' from a simple man who has seen a lot."

In the elevator Chance gazed at the small portable TV set built into a side panel. THIS EVENING was still going strong. The host was now talking to another guest, a heavily bearded singer, and Chance once again heard his name mentioned.

Upstairs, Chance was met by Rand's secretary: "That was a truly remarkable performance, sir," the woman said. "I have never seen anyone more at ease, or truer to himself. Thank goodness, we still have people like you in this country. Oh, and by the way, Mr. Rand saw you on television and though he's not feeling too well he insisted that when you got back you pay him a visit."

Chance entered Rand's bedroom. "Chauncey," said Rand, struggling to prop himself up in his enormous bed. "Let me congratulate you most warmly! Your speech was so good, so good. I hope the whole country watched you." He smoothed his blanket. "You have the great gift . . . of being natural, and that, my dear man, is a rare talent, and the true mark of a leader. You were strong and brave, yet you did not moralize. Everything you said was directly to the point."

The two men regarded each other silently.

"Chauncey, my dear friend," Rand went on, in a serious and almost reverential manner. "You will be interested in the fact that EE is chairman of the Hospitality Committee of the United Nations. It is only right that she should be present at the U.N. reception tomorrow. Since I won't be able to escort her, I would like you to do so for me. Your speech will be uppermost in many people's minds, and many, I know, would like very much to meet you. You will escort her, won't you?"

"Yes. Of course I'll be glad to accompany EE."

For a moment, Rand's face seemed blurred, as if it were frozen inwardly. He moistened his lips; his eyes aimlessly scanned the room. Then he focused them on Chance. "Thank you, Chauncey. And . . . by the way," he said quietly, "if anything should happen to me, please do take care of her. She needs someone like you . . . very much."

They shook hands and said good-bye. Chance went to his room.

$$* \quad * \quad *$$

On the plane back to New York from Denver, EE thought more and more about Gardiner. She tried to discover a unifying thread in the events of the last two days. She remembered that when she first saw him after the accident, he did not seem surprised; his face was without expression, his manner calm and detached. He behaved as if he had expected the accident, the pain, and even her appearance.

Two days had passed, but she did not know who he was and where he had come from. He steadily avoided any talk about himself. The day before, while the servants were eating in the kitchen and Chance was asleep, she had carefully gone through all of his belongings, but there were no documents among them, no checks, no money, no credit cards; she was not able to find even the stray stub of a theater ticket. It puzzled her that he traveled this way. Presumably, his personal affairs were attended to by a business or a bank which remained at his instant disposal. For he was obviously well-to-do. His suits were hand-tailored from an exquisite cloth, his shirts handmade from the most delicate silks and his shoes handmade from the softest leather. His suitcase was almost new, though its shape and lock were of an old-fashioned design.

On several occasions she had attempted to question him about his past. He had resorted to one or another of his favorite comparisons drawn on television or taken from nature; she guessed that he was troubled by a business loss, or even a bankruptcy—so common nowadays—or perhaps by the loss of a woman's love. Perhaps he had decided to leave the woman on the spur of the moment and was still wondering if he should return. Somewhere in this country there was the community where he had lived, a place which contained his home, his business, and his past.

He had not dropped names; nor had he referred to places or events. Indeed, she could not remember encountering anyone who relied more on his own self. Gardiner's manner alone indicated social confidence and financial security.

She could not define the feelings that he kindled in her. She was aware that her pulse raced when she was near him, aware of his image in her thoughts and of the difficulty she had in speaking to him in cool, even tones. She wanted to know him, and she wanted to yield to that knowledge. There were innumerable selves that he evoked in her. Yet she was not able to discover a single motive in any of his actions, and for a brief instant she feared him. From the beginning, she noticed the meticulous care he took to insure that nothing he said to her or to anyone else was definite enough to reveal what he thought of her or of anyone or, indeed, of anything.

But unlike the other men with whom she was intimate, Gardiner neither restrained nor repulsed her. The thought of seducing him, of making him lose his composure, excited her. The more withdrawn he was, the more she wanted him to look at her and to acknowledge her desire, to recognize her as a willing mistress. She saw herself making love to him—abandoned, wanton, without reticence or reserve.

She arrived home late that evening and called Chance, asking him whether she could come to his room. He agreed.

She looked tired. "I am so sorry I had to be away. I missed your television appearance—and I missed you," she murmured in a timid voice.

She sat down on the edge of the bed; Chance moved back to give her more room.

She brushed her hair from her forehead, and, looking at him quietly, put her hand on his arm. "Please don't . . . run away from me! Don't!" She sat motionless, her head resting against Chance's shoulder.

Chance was bewildered: there was clearly no place to which he could run away. He searched his memory and recalled situations on TV in which a woman advanced toward a man on a couch or a bed or inside a car. Usually, after a while, they would come very close to each other, and, often they would be partly undressed. They would then kiss and embrace. But on TV what happened next was always obscured: a brand-new image would appear on the screen: the embrace of man and woman was utterly forgotten. And yet, Chance knew, there could be other gestures and other kinds of closeness following such intimacies. Chance had just a fleeting memory of a maintenance man who, years ago, used to come to the Old Man's house to take care of the incinerator. On several occasions, after he was through with the work, he would come out into the garden and drink beer. Once he showed Chance a number of small photographs of a man and woman who were completely naked. In one of these photographs, a woman held the man's unnaturally long and thickened organ in her hand. In another, the organ was lost between her legs.

As the maintenance man talked about the photographs and what they portrayed, Chance scrutinized them closely. The images on paper were vaguely disturbing; on television he had never seen the unnaturally enlarged hidden parts of men and women, or these freakish embraces. When the maintenance man left, Chance stooped down to look over his own body. His organ was small and limp; it did not protrude in the slightest. The maintenance man insisted that in this organ hidden seeds grew, and that they came forth in a spurt whenever a man took his pleasure. Though Chance prodded and massaged his organ, he felt nothing; even in the early morning, when he woke up and often found it somewhat enlarged, his organ refused to stiffen out: it gave him no pleasure at all.

Later, Chance tried hard to figure out what connection there was—if any—between a woman's private parts and the birth of a child. In some of the TV series about doctors and hospitals and operations, Chance had often seen the mystery of birth depicted: the pain and agony of the mother, the joy of the father, the pink, wet body of the newborn infant. But he had never watched any show which explained why some women had babies and others did not. Once or twice Chance was tempted to ask Louise about it, but he decided against it. Instead, he watched TV, for a while, with closer attention. Eventually, he forgot about it.

EE had begun to smooth his shirt. Her hand was warm; now it touched his chin. Chance did not move. "I am sure . . ." EE whispered, "you must . . . you do know that I want us, want you and me to become very close. . . ." Suddenly, she began to cry quietly, like a child. Sobbing and blowing her nose, she took out her handkerchief and patted her eyes; but still she kept on crying.

Chance assumed that he was in some way responsible for her sorrow, but he did not know how. He put his arms around EE. She, as if expecting his touch, leaned heavily against him, and they tumbled over together on the bed. EE bent over his chest, her hair brushing his face. She kissed his neck and forehead; she kissed his eyes and his ears. Her tears wet his skin, and Chance smelled her perfume, all the while thinking of what he should do next. Now EE's hand touched his waist, and Chance felt the hand exploring his thighs. After a while, the hand withdrew. EE was not crying any longer; she lay quietly next to him, still and peaceful.

"I am grateful to you, Chauncey," she said. "You are a man of restraint. You know that with one touch of your hand, just one touch, I would open to you. But you do not wish to exploit another," she reflected. "In some ways you are not really American. You are more of a European man, do you know that?" She smiled. "What I mean is that, unlike men I have known, you do not practice all of those American lovers'-lane tricks, all of that fingering, kissing, tickling, stroking, hugging: that coy meandering toward the target, which is both feared and desired." She paused. "Do you know that you're very brainy, very cerebral, really, Chauncey, that you want to conquer the woman from within her very own self, that you want to infuse in her the need and the desire and the longing for your love?"

Chance was confused when she said that he wasn't really American. Why should she say that? On TV, he had often seen the dirty, hairy, noisy men and women who openly declared themselves anti-American, or were declared so by police, well-dressed officials of the government and businessmen, neat people who called themselves American. On TV, these confrontations often ended in violence, bloodshed, and death.

EE stood up and rearranged her clothes. She looked at him; there was no enmity in her look. "I might just as well tell you this, Chauncey," she said. "I am in love with you. I love you, and I want you. And I know that you know it, and I am grateful that you have decided to wait until . . . until . . ." She searched, but could not find the words. She left the room. Chance got up and patted down his hair. He sat by his desk and turned on the TV. The image appeared instantly.

Five

It was Thursday. As soon as he opened his eyes, Chance turned on the TV, then called the kitchen for his breakfast.

The maid brought in the neatly arranged breakfast tray. She told him that Mr. Rand had had a relapse, that two additional doctors had been summoned, and that they had been at his bedside since midnight. She handed Chance a pile of newspapers and a typed note. Chance did not know whom the note was from.

He had just finished eating when EE called. "Chauncey—darling—did you get my note? And did you see this morning's papers?" she asked. "It seems you've been described as one of the chief architects of the President's policy speech. And your own comments on THIS EVENING are quoted side by side with the President's. Oh, Chauncey, you were marvelous! Even the President was impressed by you!"

"I like the President," said Chance.

"I hear you looked absolutely smashing on TV! All my friends want to meet you. Chauncey, you are still going to the U.N. reception with me this afternoon?"

"Yes, I'd be happy to go."

"You are a dear. I hope you won't find all the fuss too boring. We don't have to stay late. After the reception we can go and see some friends of mine if you like; they're giving a large dinner party."

"I'll be glad to go with you."

"Oh, I'm so happy," EE exclaimed. Her voice dropped: "Can I see you? I've missed you so very much. . . ."

"Yes, of course."

She entered the room, her face flushed. "I have to tell you something that's very important to me, and I must say it as I look at you," she said, catching her breath and stopping to grope for words. "I wonder if you would consider remaining here with us, Chauncey, at least for a while. This invitation is Ben's as well as mine." She did not wait for an answer. "Think of it! You can live here in this house with us! Chauncey, please, don't say no! Benjamin is so ill; he said he feels so much more secure with you under the same roof." She threw her arms around him and pressed her body hard against his. "Chauncey, my dearest, you must, you must," she whispered. There was an unguarded quaver in her voice.

Chance agreed.

EE hugged him and kissed his cheek; then she broke away from him and began circling the room. "I know! We must get you a secretary. Now that you are in the public eye, you'll want someone experienced to help you with your affairs and screen your callers, to protect you from the people you don't want to talk to or meet. But perhaps there's someone you already have in mind? Someone who's worked for you in the past?"

"No," Chance answered. "There's no one."

"Then I'll start looking for someone right away," she said huskily.

Before lunch, while Chance was watching TV, EE rang his room. "Chauncey, I hope I'm not disturbing you," she said in a measured voice. "But I would like you to meet Mrs. Aubrey, who is here in the library with me. She would like to be considered for the post of temporary secretary until we can find a permanent one. Can you see her now?"

"Yes, I can," said Chance.

When Chance entered the library, he saw a gray-haired woman sitting beside EE on the sofa.

EE introduced them.

Chance shook hands and sat down. Under the inquisitive stare of Mrs. Aubrey, he drummed his fingers on the desk top. "Mrs. Aubrey has been Mr. Rand's trusted secretary at the First American Financial Corporation for years," EE exclaimed.

"I see," Chance said.

"Mrs. Aubrey does not want to retire—she's certainly not the type for that." Chance had nothing to say. He rubbed his thumb over his cheek. EE pulled up her wristwatch, which had slipped down on her hand.

"If you'd like, Chauncey," EE continued, "Mrs. Aubrey can make herself available immediately. . . ."

"Good," he said, finally. "I hope Mrs. Aubrey will enjoy working here. This is a fine household."

EE sought his glance across the desk. "In that case," she said, "it's settled. I've got to run now. I have to get dressed for the reception. I'll speak to you later, Chauncey."

Chance watched Mrs. Aubrey. She had turned her head to one side and seemed almost wistful. She resembled a solitary dandelion.

He liked her. He did not know what to say. He waited for Mrs. Aubrey to speak. At length, she caught his stare and said softly: "Perhaps we can start. If you would care to give me an outline of the general nature of your business and social activities . . ."

"Please speak to Mrs. Rand about it," said Chance, rising.

Mrs. Aubrey hastily got to her feet. "I quite understand," she said. "In any case, sir, I am at your disposal. My office is just next to that of Mr. Rand's private secretary."

Chance said, "Thank you again," and walked out of the room.

*   *   *

At the United Nations fete, Chance and EE were greeted by members of the U.N. Hospitality Committee and escorted to one of the most prominent tables. The Secretary-General approached; he greeted EE by kissing her hand and asking about Rand's health. Chance could not recall ever having seen the man on TV.

"This," said EE to the Secretary-General, "is Mr. Chauncey Gardiner, a very dear friend of Benjamin's."

The men shook hands. "I know this gentleman," the Secretary said, still smiling. "I admired Mr. Gardiner so much on television last night. I am honored by your presence here, sir."

They all sat down; waiters arrived with canapés of caviar, salmon, and egg, and trays crowded with glasses of champagne; photographers hovered about and snapped pictures. A tall florid man approached the table, and the Secretary-General rose like a shot. "Mr. Ambassador," he said, "how good of you to come over." He turned to EE. "May I have the honor of introducing His Excellency Vladimir Skrapinov, Ambassador of the Union of Soviet Socialist Republics?"

"Mr. Ambassador and I have already had the pleasure of meeting, haven't we?" EE smiled. "I recall a warm exchange between Mr. Rand and Ambassador Skrapinov two years ago in Washington." She paused. "Unfortunately, Mr. Rand is ill and must forgo the pleasure of your company here today." The Ambassador bowed cordially, seated himself, and talked loudly with EE and the Secretary-General. Chance fell silent and looked over the crowd. After a time the Secretary-General rose, reaffirmed his pleasure at meeting Chance, said good-bye, and departed. EE caught sight of her old friend, the Ambassador of Venezuela, who was just passing by, excused herself and went over to him.

The Soviet Ambassador moved his chair closer to Chance's. The flashbulbs of the photographers flashed away. "I'm sorry we didn't meet sooner," he said. "I saw you on THIS EVENING and must say that I listened with great interest to your down-to-earth philosophy. I'm not surprised that it was so quickly endorsed by your President." He drew his chair still closer. "Tell me, Mr. Gardiner, how is our mutual friend, Benjamin Rand? I hear that his illness is actually very serious. I did not want to upset Mrs. Rand by discussing it in detail."

"He's ill," Chance said. "He's not well at all."

"So I understand, so I've heard." The Ambassador nodded, looking intently at Chance. "Mr. Gardiner," he said, "I want to be candid. Considering the gravity of your country's economic situation, it is clear that you will be called upon to play an important role in the administration. I have detected in you a certain . . . reticence regarding political issues. But, Mr. Gardiner, after all . . . shouldn't we, the diplomats, and you, the businessmen, get together more often? We are not so far from each other, not so far!"

Chance touched his forehead with his hand. "We are not," he said. "Our chairs are almost touching."

The Ambassador laughed aloud. The photographers clicked. "Bravo, very good!" the Ambassador exclaimed. "Our chairs are indeed almost touching! And —how shall I put it—we both want to remain seated on them, don't we? Neither of us wants his chair snatched from under him, am I right? Am I correct?

Good! Excellent! Because if one goes, the other goes and then—boom!—we are both down, and no one wants to be down before his time, eh?" Chance smiled, and the Ambassador laughed loudly once again.

Skrapinov suddenly bent toward him. "Tell me, Mr. Gardiner, do you by any chance like Krylov's fables? I ask this because you have that certain Krylovian touch."

Chance looked around and saw that he and Skrapinov were being filmed by cameramen. "Krylovian touch? Do I really?" he asked and smiled.

"I knew it, I knew it!" Skrapinov almost shouted. "So you know Krylov!" The Ambassador paused and then spoke rapidly in another language. The words sounded soft, and the Ambassador's features took on the look of an animal. Chance, who had never been addressed in a foreign language, raised his eyebrows and then laughed. The Ambassador looked astonished. "So . . . so! I was correct, wasn't I? You do know your Krylov in Russian, don't you? Mr. Gardiner, I must confess that I suspected as much all along. I know an educated man when I meet one." Chance was about to deny it when the Ambassador winked. "I appreciate your discretion, my friend." Again he spoke to Chance in a foreign tongue; this time Chance did not react.

Just then, EE returned to the table, accompanied by two diplomats, whom she introduced as Gaufridi, a *député* from Paris, and His Excellency Count von Brockburg-Schulendorff, of West Germany. "Benjamin and I," she reminisced, "had the pleasure of visiting the Count's ancient castle near Munich. . . ."

The men were seated, and the photographers kept shooting. Von Brockburg-Schulendorff smiled, waiting for the Russian to speak. Skrapinov responded by smiling. Gaufridi looked from EE to Chance.

"Mr. Gardiner and I," began Skrapinov, "have just been sharing our enthusiasm for Russian fables. It appears that Mr. Gardiner is an avid reader and admirer of our poetry, which, incidentally, he reads in the original."

The German pulled his chair closer to Chance's. "Allow me to say, Mr. Gardiner, how much I admired your naturalistic approach to politics and economics on television. Of course, now that I know you have a literary background, I feel that I can understand your remarks much better." He looked at the Ambassador, then lifted his eyes to the ceiling. "Russian literature," he announced, "has inspired some of the greatest minds of our age."

"—Not to speak of German literature!" Skrapinov exclaimed. "My dear Count, may I remind you of Pushkin's lifelong admiration for the literature of your country. Why, after Pushkin translated *Faust* into Russian, Goethe sent him his own pen! Not to mention Turgenev, who settled in Germany, and the love of Tolstoy and Dostoevsky for Schiller."

Von Brockburg-Schulendorff nodded. "Yes, but can you calculate the effect of reading the Russian masters on Hauptmann, Nietzsche, and Thomas Mann? And how about Rilke: how often did Rilke declare that whatever was English was foreign to him, while whatever was Russian was his ancestral homeland . . . ?"

Gaufridi abruptly finished a glass of champagne. His face was flushed. He leaned across the table toward Skrapinov. "When we first met during World War II," he said, "you and I were dressed in soldiers' uniforms, fighting the common enemy, the cruelest enemy in the annals of our nations' histories. Sharing literary influences is one thing, sharing blood another."

Skrapinov attempted a smile. "But, Mr. Gaufridi," he said, "you speak of the time of war, many years ago—another era altogether. Today, our uniforms and decorations are on display in museums. Today, we . . . we are soldiers of peace." He had scarcely finished when Von Brockburg-Schulendorff excused himself; he rose abruptly, shoved his chair aside, kissed EE's hand, shook hands with Skrapinov and Chance, and, bowing in the direction of the Frenchman, strode off. The photographers popped away.

EE exchanged seats with the Frenchman so that he and Chance could sit next to each other. "Mr. Gardiner," the *député* began mildly, as if nothing had occurred, "I heard the President's speech, in which he referred to his consultations with you. I have read a lot about you, and I've also had the pleasure of watching you on television." He lit a long cigarette which he had carefully inserted into a holder. "I understand from the remarks of Ambassador Skrapinov that, among your many other accomplishments, you are also a man of letters." He looked sharply at Chance. "My dear Mr. Gardiner, it is only by . . . accepting fables as reality sometimes that we can advance a little way along the path of power and peace. . . ." Chance lifted his glass. "It will come as no surprise to you," he went on, "that many of our own industrialists, financiers, and members of government have the keenest interest in developments of the First American Financial Corporation. Ever since the illness of our mutual friend, Benjamin, their view of the course which the Corporation will pursue has been somewhat . . . shall we say, obstructed." He halted, but Chance said nothing. "We are pleased to hear that you may fill Rand's place, should Benjamin fail to get well. . . ."

"Benjamin will get well," said Chance. "The President said so."

"Let us hope so," declared the Frenchman. "Let us hope. And yet none of us, not even the President, can be sure. Death hovers nearby, always ready to swoop down. . . ."

Gaufridi was interrupted by the departure of the Soviet Ambassador. Everyone stood up. Skrapinov edged toward Chance. "A most interesting meeting, Mr. Gardiner," he said quietly. "Most instructive. If you should ever visit our country, my government would be most honored to offer you its hospitality." He pressed Chance's hand while film cameras rolled and photographers took photographs.

Gaufridi sat with Chance and EE at the table.

"Chauncey," said EE, "you must have really impressed our stiff Russian friend! A pity Benjamin couldn't have been here—he so enjoys talking politics!" She put her head closer to Chance. "It's no secret that you were talking Russian to Skrapinov—I didn't know you knew the language! That's incredible!"

Gaufridi sputtered: "It's extremely useful to speak Russian these days. Are you proficient in other languages, Mr. Gardiner?"

"Mr. Gardiner's a modest man," EE blurted out. "He doesn't advertise his accomplishments! His knowledge is for himself!"

A tall man approached to pay his respects to EE: Lord Beauclerk, chairman of the board of the British Broadcasting Company. He turned toward Chance.

"I enormously enjoyed the bluntness of your statement on television. Very cunning of you, very cunning indeed! One doesn't want to work things out too finely, does one? I mean—not for the videots. It's what they want, after all: *'a god to punish, not a man of their infirmity.'* Eh?"

As they were about to leave, they found themselves surrounded by men carrying open tape recorders and motion picture and portable TV cameras. One after the other, EE introduced them to Chance. One of the younger reporters stepped forward. "Would you be so kind as to answer a few questions, Mr. Gardiner?"

EE stepped in front of Chance. "Let's get this straight right now," she said. "You will not keep Mr. Gardiner too long; he must leave soon. Agreed?"

A reporter called out: "What do you think of the editorial on the President's speech in the New York *Times?*"

Chance looked at EE, but she returned his inquiring glance. He had to say something. "I didn't read it," he declared.

"You didn't read the *Times* editorial on the President's address?"

"I did not," said Chance.

Several journalists exchanged leers. EE gazed at Chance with mild astonishment, and then with growing admiration.

"But, sir," one of the reporters persisted coldly, "you must at least have glanced at it."

"I did not read the *Times*," Chance repeated.

"The *Post* spoke of your 'peculiar brand of optimism,' " said another man. "Did you read that?"

"No. I didn't read that either."

"Well," the reporter persisted, "what about the phrase, 'peculiar brand of optimism'?"

"I don't know what it means," Chance replied.

EE stepped forward proudly. "Mr. Gardiner has many responsibilities," she said, "especially since Mr. Rand has been ill. He finds out what is in the newspapers from the staff briefings."

An older reporter stepped forward. "I am sorry to persist, Mr. Gardiner, but it would nonetheless be of great interest to me to know which newspapers you 'read,' so to speak, via your staff briefings."

"I do not read any newspapers," said Chance. "I watch TV."

The journalists stood, silent and embarrassed. "Do you mean," one finally asked, "that you find TV's coverage more objective than that of the newspapers?"

"As I've said," explained Chance, "I watch TV."

The older reporter half-turned away. "Thank you,

Mr. Gardiner," he said, "for what is probably the most honest admission to come from a public figure in recent years. Few men in public life have had the courage not to read newspapers. None have had the guts to admit it!"

As EE and Chance were about to leave the building, they were overtaken by a young woman photographer. "I am sorry for pursuing you, Mr. Gardiner," she said breathlessly, "but can I have just one more picture of you—you're a very photogenic man, you know!"

Chance smiled at her politely; EE recoiled slightly. Chance was surprised by her anger. He did not know what had upset her.

✳   ✳   ✳

The President casually glanced at the press digest of the day before. All the major papers reported the text of his speech at the Financial Institute of America and included his remarks about Benjamin Rand and Chauncey Gardiner. It occurred to the President that he ought to know more about Gardiner.

He called his personal secretary and asked her to gather all available information about Gardiner. Later, between appointments, he summoned her to his office.

The President took the file she handed him. He

opened it, found a complete dossier on Rand, which he immediately laid aside, a brief interview with Rand's chauffeur sketchily describing Gardiner's accident and a transcript of Gardiner's remarks on THIS EVENING.

"There seems to be no other information, Mr. President," his secretary said hesitantly.

"All I want is the usual material we always get before inviting guests to the White House; that's all."

The secretary fidgeted uneasily. "I did consult our standard sources, Mr. President, but they don't seem to contain anything on Mr. Chauncey Gardiner."

The President's brows knitted and he said icily: "I assume that Mr. Chauncey Gardiner, like all the rest of us, was born of certain parents, grew up in certain places, made certain connections, and like the rest of us contributed, through his taxes, to the wealth of this nation. And so, I'm sure, did his family. Just give me the basics, please."

The secretary looked uncomfortable. "I'm sorry, Mr. President, but I wasn't able to find out anything more than what I've just given you. As I said, I did try all of our usual sources."

"You mean to say," the President muttered gravely, pointing tensely at the file, "that this is absolutely all they have on him?"

"That is correct, sir."

"Am I to assume that none of our agencies knows a single thing about a man with whom I spent half an hour, face-to-face, and whose name and words I quoted in my speech? Have you by any chance tried *Who's Who?* And, for God's sake, if that fails, try the Manhattan telephone book!"

The secretary laughed nervously. "I'll keep trying, sir."

"I certainly would appreciate it if you would."

The secretary left the room, and the President reached for his calendar and scribbled in its margin: *Gardiner?*

＊　　＊　　＊

Immediately after leaving the United Nations reception, Ambassador Skrapinov prepared a secret report about Gardiner. Chauncey Gardiner, he maintained, was shrewd, and highly educated. He emphasized Gardiner's knowledge of Russian and of Russian literature, and saw in Gardiner "the spokesman of those American business circles which, in view of deepening depression and widening civil unrest, were bent on maintaining their threatened *status quo*, even at the price of political and economic concessions to the Soviet bloc."

At home, in the Soviet Mission to the United Nations, the Ambassador telephoned his embassy in Washington and spoke to the chief of the Special Section. He requested, on a top-priority basis, all information concerning Gardiner: he wanted details on his family, education, his friends and associates, and his relationship with Rand, and he wanted to find out the real reason why, of all his economic advisers, the President had singled him out. The chief of the Special Section promised to deliver a complete dossier by the following morning.

Next, the Ambassador personally supervised the preparation of small gift packages to be delivered to Gardiner and Rand. Each package contained several pounds of Beluga caviar and bottles of specially distilled Russian vodka. In addition, he had a rare first edition of Krylov's *Fables*, with Krylov's own notes handwritten on many of the pages, inserted into Gardiner's package. The volume had been requisitioned from the private collection of a recently arrested Jewish member of the Academy of Sciences in Leningrad.

Later, as he was shaving, the Ambassador decided to take a chance: he decided to include Gardiner's name in the speech that he was to deliver that evening to the International Congress of the Mercantile Association, convening in Philadelphia. The paragraph, introduced into the speech after it had already been approved by his superiors in Moscow, welcomed the emergence in the United States of "those enlightened statesmen—personified by, among others, Mr. Chauncey Gardiner—who are clearly aware that, unless the leaders of the opposing political systems move the chairs on which they sit closer to each other, all of their seats will be pulled out from under them by rapid social and political changes."

Skrapinov's speech was a hit. The allusion to Gardiner was picked up by the major news media. At midnight, watching TV, Skrapinov heard his speech quoted and saw a close-up of Gardiner—a man who, according to the announcer, had been "within the space of two days cited by both the President of the United States and the Soviet Ambassador to the United Nations."

On the frontispiece of Krylov's works, the Ambassador had inscribed: " *'One could make this fable clearer still: but let us not provoke the geese' (Krylov). —To Mr. Chauncey Gardiner, with admiration and in the hope of future meetings, warmly, Skrapinov.*"

* * *

After arriving at the home of EE's friends from the United Nations, EE and Chance found themselves in a room that was at least three stories high; at half its height along the wall ran the ornately carved balustrade of a gallery. The room was full of sculptures and glass cases containing shiny objects; the chandelier, hanging on a golden rope, resembled a tree whose leaves had been replaced by flickering candles.

Groups of guests were scattered around the room, and the waiters circulated with trays of drinks. The hostess, a fat woman in a green gown, with thick strings of jewels on her exposed chest, walked toward them, arms outstretched. She and EE embraced and kissed each other on the cheek; then EE introduced Chance. The woman put out her hand and held Chance's for a moment. "At last, at last," she exclaimed cheerfully, "the famous Chauncey Gardiner! EE has told me that you cherish your privacy more than anything else." She stopped, as if a more profound second thought had come to her, then threw back her head a bit and measured him up and down. "But now, when I see how good-looking you are, I suspect it has been EE who cherishes her privacy— with you!"

"Sophie, dear," EE pleaded coyly.

"I know, I know. Suddenly, you are embarrassed! There is nothing wrong with being fond of one's privacy, EE, dear!" She laughed and, with her hand on Chance's arm, continued gaily: "Please, do forgive me, Mr. Gardiner. EE and I always joke like this when we're together. You look even handsomer than your photographs, and I must say I agree with *Women's Wear Daily*—you're obviously one of the best-dressed businessmen today. Of course, with your height and broad shoulders and narrow hips and long legs and . . ."

"Sophie, please—" EE broke in, blushing.

"I'll be quiet now, I will. Do follow me, both of you; let's meet some interesting people. Everybody is so anxious to talk to Mr. Gardiner."

Chance was introduced to a number of guests. He shook their hands, met the stares of women and men, and, barely catching their names, gave his own. A short, bald man succeeded in cornering him next to an imposing piece of furniture, full of sharp edges.

"I'm Ronald Stiegler, of Eidolon Books. Delighted to meet you, sir." The man extended his hand. "We watched your TV performance with great interest," said Stiegler. "And just now, coming over here in my car, I heard on the radio that the Soviet Ambassador mentioned your name in Philadelphia . . ."

"On your radio? Don't you have television in your car?" Chance asked. Stiegler pretended to be amused. "I hardly even listen to my radio. With traffic so hectic, one has to pay attention to everything." He stopped a waiter and asked for a vodka martini on the rocks with a twist of orange.

"I've been thinking," he said, leaning against the wall, "and so have some of my editors: Would you consider writing a book for us? Something on your special subject. Clearly, the view from the White House is different from the view of the egghead or the hardhat. What do you say?" He drained off his drink in several gulps and when a servant passed by carrying a tray of glasses, grabbed another. "One for you?" He grinned at Chance.

"No, thank you. I don't drink."

"Sir, I'm thinking: it would be only fair and it would certainly be to the country's advantage to promote your philosophy more widely. Eidolon Books would be very happy to perform this service for you. Right here and now I think I could promise you a six-figure advance against royalties and a very agreeable royalty and reprint clause. The contract could be drawn up and signed in a day or two, and you could have the book for us, let's say, in about a year or two."

"I can't write," said Chance.

Stiegler smiled deprecatingly. "Of course—but who can, nowadays? It's no problem. We can provide you with our best editors and research assistants. I can't even write a simple postcard to my children. So what?"

"I can't even read," said Chance.

"Of course not!" Stiegler exclaimed. "Who has

time? One glances at things, talks, listens, watches. Mr. Gardiner, I admit that as a publisher I should be the last one to tell you this . . . but publishing isn't exactly a flowering garden these days."

"What kind of garden is it?" asked Chance with interest.

"Well, whatever it was once, it isn't any more. Of course, we're still growing, still expanding. But too many books are being published. And what with recession, stagnation, unemployment . . . Well, as you must know, books aren't selling any more. But, as I say, for a tree of your height, there is still a sizable plot reserved. Yes, I can see a Chauncey Gardiner blooming under the Eidolon imprint! Let me drop you a little note, outlining our thoughts and—our figures. Are you still at the Rands'?"

"Yes, I am."

Dinner was announced. The guests were seated around several small tables arranged symmetrically throughout the dining room. There were ten at Chance's table; he was flanked on each side by a woman. The conversation quickly turned to politics. An older man sitting across from Chance addressed him, and Chance stiffened uneasily.

"Mr. Gardiner, when is the government going to stop calling industrial by-products poisons? I went along with the banning of DDT because DDT is a poison and there's no problem finding some new chemicals. But it's a damn sight different when we stop the manufacture of heating oils, let's say, because we don't like the decomposition products of kerosene!" Chance stared silently at the old man. "I say, by God, that there's a helluva difference between petroleum ash and bug powder! Any idiot could see that!"

"I have seen ashes and I have seen powders," said Chance. "I know that both are bad for growth in a garden."

"Hear, hear!" the woman sitting on Chance's right cried out. "He's marvelous!" she whispered to the companion on her right in a voice loud enough for everyone to hear. To the others, she said: "Mr. Gardiner has the uncanny ability of reducing complex matters to the simplest of human terms. But by bringing this down to earth, to our own home," the woman continued, "I can see the priority and urgency which Mr. Gardiner and the influential men like him, including our President, who quotes him so often, give to this matter." Several of the others smiled.

A distinguished-looking man in pince-nez addressed Chance: "All right, Mr. Gardiner," he said, "the President's speech was reassuring. Still and all, these are the facts: unemployment is approaching catastrophic proportions, unprecedented in this country; the market continues to fall toward 1929 levels; some of the largest and finest companies in our country have collapsed. Tell me, sir, do you honestly believe that the President will be able to halt this downward trend?"

"Mr. Rand said that the President knows what he is doing," said Chance slowly. "They spoke; I was there; that is what Mr. Rand said after they were finished."

"What about the war?" the young woman sitting on Chance's left said, leaning close to him.

"The war? Which war?" said Chance. "I've seen many wars on TV."

"Alas," the woman said, "in this country, when we dream of reality, television wakes us. To millions, the war, I suppose, is just another TV program. But out there, at the front, real men are giving their lives."

While Chance sipped coffee in one of the adjoining sitting rooms, he was discreetly approached by one of the guests. The man introduced himself and sat down next to Chance, regarding him intently. He was older than Chance. He looked like some of the men Chance often saw on TV. His long silky gray hair was combed straight from his forehead to the nape of his neck. His eyes were large and expressive and shaded with unusually long eyelashes. He talked softly and from time to time uttered a short dry laugh. Chance did not understand what he said or why he laughed. Every time he felt that the man expected an answer from him, Chance said yes. More often, he simply smiled and nodded. Suddenly, the man bent over and whispered a question to which he wanted a definite answer. Yet Chance was not certain what he had asked and so gave no reply. The man repeated himself. Again Chance remained silent. The man leaned still closer and looked at him hard; apparently, he caught something in Chance's expression which made him ask, in a cold toneless voice: "Do you want to do it now? We can go upstairs and do it."

Chance did not know what the man wanted him to do. What if it were something he couldn't do? Finally he said, "I would like to watch."

"Watch? You mean, watch me? Just doing it alone?" The man made no effort to hide his amazement.

"Yes," said Chance, "I like to watch very much." The man averted his eyes and then turned to Chance once more. "If that's what you want, then I want it too," he declared boldly.

After liqueurs were served, the man gazed into Chance's eyes and impatiently slid his hand under Chance's arm. With his surprisingly strong forearm he pressed Chance to him. "It's time for us," he whispered. "Let's go upstairs."

Chance did not know if he should leave without letting EE know where he was going.

"I want to tell EE," Chance said.

The man stared wildly at him. "Tell EE?" He paused. "I see. Well, it's all the same: tell her later."

"Not now?"

"Please," said the man. "Let's go. She'll never miss you in this crowd. We'll walk casually down to the rear elevator and go straight upstairs. Do come with me."

They moved through the crowded room. Chance looked around, but EE was not in sight.

The elevator was narrow, its walls covered with soft purple fabric. The man stood next to Chance and suddenly thrust his hand into Chance's groin. Chance did not know what to do. The man's face was friendly; there was an eager look on it. His hand continued to probe Chance's trousers. Chance decided that the best thing was to do nothing.

The elevator stopped. The man got out first and led Chance by the arm. All was quiet. They entered a bedroom. The man asked Chance to sit down. He opened a small concealed bar and offered Chance a drink. Chance was afraid that he might pass out as he had done that time in the car with EE; therefore he refused. He also refused to smoke a strange-smelling pipe which the man offered him. The man poured himself a large drink, which he drank almost at once. Then he approached Chance and embraced him, pressing his thighs against Chance's. Chance remained still. The man now kissed his neck and cheeks, then sniffed and mussed his hair. Chance wondered what he had said or done to prompt such affection. He tried very hard to recall seeing something like this on TV but could remember only a single scene in a film in which a man kissed another man. Even then it had not been clear what was actually happening. He remained still.

The man clearly did not mind this; his eyes were closed, his lips parted. He slipped his hands under Chance's jacket, searching insistently; then he stepped away, looked at Chance, and, hurrying, began to undress. He kicked off his shoes and lay naked on the bed. He gestured to Chance: Chance stood beside the bed and looked down at the prostrate form. To Chance's surprise, the man cupped his own flesh in a hand, groaning and jerking and trembling as he did so.

The man was certainly ill. Chance often saw people having fits on TV. He leaned over and the man suddenly grabbed him. Chance lost his balance and almost fell upon the naked body. The man reached for Chance's leg, and without a word raised and pressed the sole of Chance's shoe against his hardened organ.

Seeing how the erect extended part grew stiffer under the edge of his shoe and how it protruded from the man's underbelly, Chance recalled the photographs of the man and woman shown to him by the maintenance man in the Old Man's house. He felt uneasy. But he lent his foot to the man's flesh, watched the man's body tremble and saw how his naked legs stretched out, straining tautly, and heard how he screamed out of some inner agony. And then the man again pressed Chance's shoe into his flesh. From under the shoe a white substance coursed forth in short spurts. The man's face went pale: his head jerked from side to side. The man twitched for the last time; the trembling and shivering of his body subsided and his muscles tensed under Chance's shoe, calmed and softened as if they had been suddenly unplugged from a source of energy. He closed his eyes. Chance reclaimed his foot and quietly left.

He found his way back to the elevator and on the ground floor walked down a long corridor, guided by the sound of voices. Soon he was back among the guests. He was searching for EE when someone tapped him on the shoulder. It was she.

"I was afraid you got bored and left," she said. "Or that you were kidnaped. There are loads of women here who wouldn't mind making off with you, you know."

Chance did not know why anyone would want to kidnap him. He was silent and finally said, "I wasn't with a woman. I was with a man. We went upstairs but he got sick and so I came down."

"Upstairs? Chauncey, you're always engaged in

some kind of discussion; I do wish you'd just relax and enjoy the party."

"He got sick," said Chance. "I stayed with him for a while."

"Very few men are as healthy as you are; they can't take all this drinking and chattering," said EE. "You're an angel, my dear. Thank God there are still men like you around to give aid and comfort."

*　　*　　*

When they returned from the dinner party, Chance got into bed and watched TV. The room was dark; the screen cast an uneasy light on the walls. Chance heard the door open. EE entered in her dressing gown and approached his bed.

"I couldn't sleep, Chauncey," she said. She touched his shoulder.

Chance wanted to turn off the TV and turn on the lights.

"Please, don't," said EE. "Let's stay like this."

She sat on the bed, next to him, and put her arms around her knees. "I had to see you," she said, "and I know—I know," she whispered in short bursts, "that you don't mind my coming here—to your room. You don't mind, do you?"

"I don't," Chance said.

Slowly, she moved closer; her hair brushed his face. In an instant she threw off her robe and slipped under his blanket.

She moved her body next to his, and he felt her hand run over the length of his bare chest and hip, stroking, squeezing, reaching down; he felt her fingers pressing feverishly into his skin. He extended his hand and let it slide over her neck and breasts and belly. He felt her trembling; he felt her limbs unfolding. He did not know what else to do and so he withdrew his hand. She continued to tremble and shiver, pressing his head and his face to her damp flesh, as if she wanted him to devour her. She cried out brokenly, uttered ruptured sounds, spoke in phrases which barely began, making noises that resembled animal gasps. Kissing his body over and over again, she wailed softly and began to half-moan and half-laugh, her tongue lunging down toward his flaccid flesh, her head bobbing, her legs beating together. She quivered, and he felt her wet thighs.

He wanted to tell her how much he preferred to look at her, that only by watching could he memorize her and take her and possess her. He did not know how to explain to her that he could not touch better or more fully with his hands than he could with his eyes. Seeing encompassed all at once; a touch was limited to one spot at a time. EE should no more have

wanted to be touched by him than should the TV screen
have wanted it.

Chance neither moved nor resisted. Suddenly EE
went limp and let her head fall on his chest. "You
don't want me," she said. "You don't feel anything
for me. Nothing at all."

Chance gently pushed her aside and sat up heavily
at the edge of the bed.

"I know, I know," she cried. "I don't excite you!"
Chance did not know what she meant. "I'm right,
aren't I, Chauncey?"

He turned and looked at her. "I like to watch you,"
he said.

She stared at him. "To watch me?"

"Yes. I like to watch."

She sat up, breathless, gasping for air. "Is that why
. . . is that all you want, to watch me?"

"Yes. I like to watch you."

"But aren't you excited?" She reached down and
took his flesh and held it in her hand. In turn, Chance
touched her; his fingers moved inside her. She jerked
again, turned her head to him, and in a fiery attempt
pulled and sucked his flesh into her mouth, licking
it with her tongue, nibbling at it with her teeth, trying desperately to breathe life into it. Chance waited
patiently until she stopped.

She wept bitterly. "You don't love me," she cried. "You can't stand it when I touch you!"

"I like to watch you," said Chance.

"I don't understand what you mean," she moaned. "No matter what I do, I can't arouse you. And you keep saying that you like to watch me. . . . Watch me! You mean . . . when . . . when I'm alone . . . ?"

"Yes. I like to watch you."

In the bluish light emanating from the TV, EE looked at him, her eyes veiled. "You want me to come while you watch."

Chance said nothing.

"If I touched myself, you'd get excited and then you'd make love to me?"

Chance did not understand. "I would like to watch you," he repeated.

"I think I understand now." She got up, paced swiftly up and down the room, crossing in front of the TV screen; every now and then a word escaped her lips, a word scarcely louder than her breath.

She returned to the bed. She stretched out on her back and let her hand run over her body; languidly, she spread her legs wide apart and then her hands crept froglike toward her belly. She swayed back and forth and shoved her body from side to side as if it were pricked by rough grass. Her fingers caressed her breasts, buttocks, thighs. In a quick motion, her legs and arms wrapped around Chance like a web of sprawling branches. She shook violently: a delicate tremor ran through her. She no longer stirred; she was half-asleep.

Chance covered her with the blanket. Then he changed the channels several times, keeping the sound low. They rested together in bed and he watched TV, afraid to move.

Sometime later, EE said to him: "I am so free with you. Up until the time I met you, every man I knew barely acknowledged me. I was a vessel that he could take hold of, pierce, and pollute. I was merely an aspect of somebody's love-making. Do you know what I mean?"

Chance looked at her but said nothing.

"Dearest . . . You uncoil my wants: desire flows within me, and when you watch me my passion dissolves it. You make me free. I reveal myself to myself and I am drenched and purged."

He remained silent.

EE stretched and smiled. "Chauncey, dear, I've been meaning to bring this up: Ben wants you to fly to Washington with me tomorrow and take me to the Capitol Hill Ball. I must go; I'm chairman of the

Fund-Raising Committee. You will come with me, won't you?"

"I would like to go with you," said Chance.

She cuddled up next to him and dozed off again. Chance watched TV until he too fell asleep.

Six

Mrs. Aubrey rang Chance in the morning. "Sir, I've just seen this morning's papers. You're in every one of them, and the photographs are stunning! There's one of you with Ambassador Skrapinov . . . and one with the Secretary-General . . . and another with . . . a German Count Somebody. The *Daily News* has a full page picture of you with Mrs. Rand. Even the *Village Voice* . . ."

"I don't read newspapers," said Chance.

"Well, anyway, a number of the major networks have invited you for exclusive TV appearances. Also, *Fortune, Newsweek, Life, Look, Vogue, House & Garden* want to do stories on you. The *Irish Times* called and so did *Spectator, Sunday Telegraph,* and *The Guardian;* they want a press conference. A Lord Beauclerk wanted me to inform you that the BBC is ready to fly you to London for a TV special; he hopes that you will be his house guest. The New York bureaus of *Jours de France, Der Spiegel, L'Osservatore Romano, Pravda, Neue Zürcher Zeitung* have called for appointments. Count von Brockburg-Schulendorff just called to tell you that *Stern,* of Germany, will have you on its cover; *Stern* would like to acquire world rights to your remarks on television, and they're waiting for your terms. French *L'Express* wants you to discuss the challenge of the American depression in their round-table interview: they'll pay your travel expenses. Mr. Gaufridi called twice to offer you his hospitality when you are in France. The directors of the Tokyo Stock Exchange would like you to inspect a new Japanese-made data retrieving computer . . ."

Chance interrupted: "I don't want to meet these people."

"I understand, sir. Just two final points: The *Wall Street Journal* has predicted your imminent appointment to the board of the First American Financial

122

Corporation, and they would like to have a statement from you. In my view, sir, if you could give them a prognosis at this time, you could help their stock enormously. . . ."

"I cannot give them anything."

"Very well, sir. The other thing is that the trustees of the Eastshore University would like to confer an honorary doctor of laws degree on you at this year's commencement exercises, but they want to make sure beforehand that you'll accept."

"I do not need a doctor," said Chance.

"Do you want to talk to the trustees?"

"No."

"I see. And what about the newspapers?"

"I don't like newspapers."

"Will you see the foreign correspondents?"

"I see them often enough on TV."

"Very good, sir. Oh, yes, Mrs. Rand wanted me to remind you that the Rand plane will be leaving for Washington at four o'clock. And she wanted me to inform you that you'll be staying at your hostess's home."

* * *

Karpatov, the chief of the Special Section, arrived on Friday to see Ambassador Skrapinov. He was immediately ushered into the Ambassador's office.

"There is no additional information in Gardiner's file," he said, placing a thin folder on the Ambassador's desk.

Skrapinov tossed the file to one side. "Where is the rest?" he asked crisply.

"There is no record of him anywhere, Comrade Skrapinov."

"Karpatov, I want the facts!"

Karpatov spoke haltingly: "Comrade Ambassador, I have been able to determine that the White House is eager to find out what we know about Gardiner. This should indicate that Gardiner has political importance of the first magnitude."

Skrapinov glared at Karpatov, then got up and began pacing back and forth behind his desk. "I want," he said, "from your Section one thing only: the facts about Gardiner."

Karpatov stood there sullenly. "Comrade Ambassador," he answered, "it is my duty to report that we have been unable to discover even the most elementary information about him. It is almost as if he had never existed before." The Ambassador's hand came down on his desk, and a small statuette toppled to the floor. Trembling, Karpatov stooped, picked it up and carefully put it back on the desk.

"Don't imagine," the Ambassador hissed, "that you can palm such rot off on me! I won't accept it! 'As if he had never existed'! Do you realize that Gardiner happens to be one of the most important men in this country and that this country happens to be not Soviet Georgia but the United States of America, the biggest imperialist state in the world! People like Gardiner decide the fate of millions every day! 'As if he had never existed'! Are you mad? Do you realize that I mentioned the man in my speech?" He paused, then bent forward toward Karpatov. "Unlike the people of your Section, I do not believe in twentieth-century 'dead souls'—nor do I believe in people from other planets coming down to haunt us, as they do on American television programs. I hereby demand all data on Chauncey Gardiner to be delivered to me personally within four hours!"

Hunching his shoulders, Karpatov left the room.

*   *   *

When four hours had passed and Skrapinov had still not heard from Karpatov, he decided to teach him a lesson. He summoned to his office Sulkin, ostensibly a minor official at the Mission, but actually one of the most powerful men in the Foreign Department.

Skrapinov complained bitterly to Sulkin about Karpatov's ineptitude, stressed the extraordinary importance of obtaining information on Gardiner, and asked that Sulkin help him get a clear picture of Gardiner's past.

After lunch, Sulkin arranged a private conference with Skrapinov. They proceeded to a room at the Mission known as "The Cellar," which was specially protected against listening devices. Sulkin opened his attaché case and with ceremony drew from a black folder a single blank piece of paper. Skrapinov waited expectantly.

"This, my dear Comrade, is your picture of Gardiner's past!" Sulkin growled.

Skrapinov glanced at the page, saw that it was blank, dropped it, glared at Sulkin, and said: "I don't understand, Comrade Sulkin. This page is empty. Does this mean that I am not to be entrusted with the facts about Gardiner?"

Sulkin sat down and lit a cigarette, slowly shaking the match out. "Investigating the background of Mr. Gardiner, my dear Comrade Ambassador, has apparently proven so difficult a task for the agents of the Special Section that it has already resulted in the loss of one of them, without his being able to uncover the tiniest detail of Gardiner's background!" Sulkin paused to puff on his cigarette. "It was fortunate, however, that on Wednesday night I took the precaution of photowiring to Moscow a tape of Gardiner's television appearance on THIS EVENING. This tape, you might be interested in knowing, was submitted to prompt psychiatric, neurological, and linguistic examination. With the aid of our latest-model computers, our teams have analyzed Gardiner's vocabulary, syntax, accent, gestures, facial and other characteristics. The results, my dear Skrapinov, may surprise you. It proved impossible to determine in any way whatsoever his ethnic background or to ascribe his accent to any single community in the entire United States!"

Skrapinov looked at Sulkin in bewilderment.

Smiling wanly, Sulkin continued: "Moreover, it may interest you to know that Gardiner appears to be emotionally one of the most well-adjusted American public figures to have emerged in recent years. However," Sulkin went on, "your Mr. Chauncey Gardiner remains, to all intents and purposes," and here he held up the sheet of paper by its corner, "a blank page."

"Blank page?"

"Blank page," echoed Sulkin. "Exactly. Gardiner's code name!"

Skrapinov quickly reached for a glass of water and gulped it down. "Excuse me, Comrade," he said. "But on Thursday evening when I took it upon myself to allude to Gardiner in my speech in Philadelphia, I naturally assumed that he was an established member of the Wall Street elite. After all, he was mentioned by the American President. But if, as it seems . . ."

Sulkin held up his hand. "Seems? What reason do you have to suggest that Chauncey Gardiner is not in actual fact the man whom you described?"

Skrapinov could barely mutter: "Blank page . . . the lack of any facts . . ."

Again Sulkin interrupted. "Comrade Ambassador," he said, "I am here actually to congratulate you on your perceptiveness. It is, I must tell you, our firm conviction that Gardiner is, in fact, a leading member of an American elitist faction that has for some years been planning a *coup d'état*. He must be of such great importance to this group that they have succeeded in masking every detail of his identity until his emergence Tuesday afternoon."

"Did you say *coup d'état?*" asked Skrapinov.

"I did," replied Sulkin. "Do you doubt the possibility?"

"Well, no. Certainly not. Lenin himself seems to have foreseen it."

"Good, very good," said Sulkin, snapping the lock of his attaché case. "It appears that your intuition has proven itself well-founded. Your initial decision to latch onto Gardiner has been justified. You have a good instinct, Comrade Skrapinov—a true Marxist instinct!" He got up to leave. "You will shortly receive special instructions about the attitude to adopt toward Gardiner."

128

When Sulkin had gone, Skrapinov thought: It's incredible! Billions of rubles are spent each year on clever Japanese gadgetry, on superspies trained and camouflaged for years, on reconnaissance satellites, overstaffed embassies, trade missions, cultural exchanges, bribes, and gifts—but all that matters in the end is a good Marxist instinct! He thought of Gardiner and envied him his youth, his composure, his future as a leader. *Blank Page, Blank Page—* The code name brought back to him memories of World War II, of the Partisans he had led to so many victories. Maybe diplomacy had been the wrong career for him; maybe the army would have been better. . . . But he was old.

*   *   *

On Friday afternoon, the President's secretary reported to him. "I'm sorry, Mr. President, but since yesterday, I have been able to collect only a few additional press clippings about Gardiner. They are the speech of the Soviet Ambassador, who mentioned him, and the transcript of Gardiner's interview with the press at the United Nations."

The President was annoyed. "Let's stop this! Have you asked Benjamin Rand about Gardiner?"

"I have telephoned the Rands, sir. Unfortunately,

Mr. Rand has had a serious relapse and is on power-ful sedatives. He can't talk."

"Did you speak to Mrs. Rand, then?"

"I did, sir. She was at her husband's bedside. She said only that Mr. Gardiner cherishes his privacy and that she respects this aspect of Mr. Gardiner's person-ality very much. She said that she feels—but only feels, you understand—that Mr. Gardiner intends to become much more active now that Mr. Rand is bed-ridden. But she did not connect Mr. Gardiner with any specific business or with any family situation."

"That's even less than what I read in the *Times!* What about our investigative sources? Have you talked to Steven?"

"I did, Mr. President. He hasn't been able to find a single thing. He's checked twice, and not one agency could help him. Gardiner's photograph and finger-prints were checked out, of course, just before your visit to Rand's and, having no record of any kind— as Rand's guest—he was cleared. And I guess that's really all I have to tell you."

"All right, all right. Call Grunmann. Tell him what you know, or, rather, don't know, and have him call me as soon as he gets something on Gardiner."

Grunmann called in a short time. "Mr. President, all of us here have been trying desperately. There just isn't a thing on him. The man doesn't seem to have existed until he moved into Rand's house three days ago!"

"I am very disturbed by this, very disturbed," said the President. "I want you to try again. I want you to keep on it, do you understand? And by the way, Walter: there's a TV program, isn't there, in which some ordinary Americans turn out to be really invaders from another planet? Well, Walter, I refuse to believe that I talked to one of these intruders in New York! I expect you to come up with a large file on Gardiner. If not, I warn you that I shall personally authorize an immediate investigation of those who are responsible for such a flagrant breach in our security!"

Grunmann called back. "Mr. President," he said in a low voice, "I am afraid that our initial fears are now confirmed. We have no record of this man's birth, of his parents, or of his family. We do know, however, beyond any doubt, and I can vouch for it, that he has never been in any legal trouble with any individual or any private, state, or federal organization, corporation, or agency. He was never the cause of any accident or of any damage and—aside from the Rand accident—he was never involved as a third party in any such situation. He has never been hospitalized;

he carries no insurance; nor, for that matter, can he possibly have any other documents or personal identification. He doesn't drive a car or fly a plane, and no license of any kind has ever been issued to him. He has no credit cards, no checks, no calling cards. He does not own a property in this country. . . . Mr. President, we snooped on him a bit in New York: he doesn't talk business or politics on the phone or at home. All he does is watch TV; the set is always on in his room: there's a constant racket—"

"He what?" interrupted the President. "What did you say, Walter?"

"I said he watches television—all the channels— practically all the time. Even when Mrs. Rand . . . is with him in his bedroom, sir . . ."

The President cut in sharply: "Walter, there's no excuse for such investigations, and, damn it, I don't want to know anything of that sort! Who the hell cares what Gardiner does in his bedroom?"

"I'm sorry, Mr. President, but we've had to try everything." He cleared his throat. "Sir, we have been getting quite apprehensive about this man Gardiner. We recorded his conversations at the United Nations reception, but he hardly said a thing. Frankly, sir, it has occurred to us that he might be the agent of a foreign power. But the fact of the matter is that those people almost invariably have too much documentation provided, too much American identity.

There's absolutely nothing un-American about them; it's a miracle, as the Director always says, that none of them gets elected to the highest office of this land—" Grunmann caught himself, but it was too late for him to brush off his remark.

"That's a very poor joke, Walter," the President said sternly.

"I'm sorry, sir, I didn't mean . . . I do apologize—"

"Go ahead with your report."

"Well, sir, first, we feel that Mr. Gardiner is not one of these transplants. Definitely not, and then, the Soviets have put out an alert for information on his background. I'm happy to tell you, Mr. President, that even this unprecedented display of Soviet curiosity has failed; not only were they unable to come up with anything beyond—I am not joking, Mr. President—newspaper clippings from our press, but as a result of their eagerness they broke their cover and lost one of their most able agents to us! What's more, eight other foreign powers have put Gardiner on their spying priorities lists. All I can say is that we shall keep on it, Mr. President . . . we shall continue investigating on a round-the-clock basis, sir, and I'll let you know just as soon as we come up with anything."

The President went upstairs to his apartment to rest. It's simply incredible, he thought, incredible.

Millions of dollars are allocated each year to each of these agencies, and they can't supply me with even the most rudimentary facts about a man now living in one of the best town houses of New York City as a guest of one of our most prominent businessmen. Is the Federal Government being undermined? By whom? He sighed, turned on TV, and dropped off to sleep.

Seven

The man sitting on the sofa faced the small group assembled in his suite. "Gentlemen," he began slowly, "some of you already know that Duncan has decided not to run with me. That leaves us, at present, without a candidate. My friends, we've got to announce someone soon, someone as good as Duncan, and I say this despite the distressing discoveries about Duncan's past that have unfortunately surfaced."

Schneider spoke out. "It wasn't easy to come up even with Duncan," he said, "and let's not kid ourselves . . . whom can we possibly get at this late date? Shellman is going to stay with his firm. I don't think Frank can even be considered, given his miserable record as president of the university."

"What about George?" a voice asked.

"George has just had another operation—the second in three months. He's an obvious health risk."

There was silence in the room. It was then that O'Flaherty spoke. "I think I have someone," he said quietly. "What about Chauncey Gardiner?" All eyes turned to the man on the sofa who was drinking his coffee.

"Gardiner?" the man on the sofa said. "Chauncey Gardiner? We don't really know anything about him, do we? Our people haven't been able to find out one single blessed thing. And he certainly hasn't been of any help: he hasn't said a thing about himself ever since he moved in with the Rands four days ago. . . ."

"Then I would like to state," said O'Flaherty, "that this makes me think of Gardiner as an even better bet."

"Why?" several men chorused.

O'Flaherty spoke easily: "What was the trouble with Duncan? With Frank and with Shellman, for that matter, and with so many of the others we've considered and have had to reject? The damn trouble was

138

that they all had background, too much background! A man's past cripples him: his background turns into a swamp and invites scrutiny!"

He waved his arms excitedly. "But just consider Gardiner. May I stress what you have just heard from a most authoritative voice: Gardiner has no background! And so he's not and cannot be objectionable to anyone! He's personable, well-spoken, and he comes across well on TV! And, as far as his thinking goes, he appears to be one of us. That's all. It's clear what he isn't. Gardiner is our one chance."

Schneider crushed out his cigar. "O'Flaherty just tapped something," he said. "Something big. Hmmmm . . . Gardiner, Gardiner . . ."

A waiter entered with steaming pots of fresh coffee and the discussion continued.

✳   ✳   ✳

Chance pushed his way through the throng of dancing couples toward the exit. In his eyes there lingered yet a faint, blurred image of the grand ballroom, of the trays of refreshments at the buffet, the multicolored flowers, brilliant bottles, rows upon rows of shining glasses on the table. He caught sight of EE as she was embraced by a tall, heavily decorated general. He passed through a blaze of photographers' flash-guns as through a cloud. The image of all he had seen outside the garden faded.

Chance was bewildered. He reflected and saw the withered image of Chauncey Gardiner: it was cut by the stroke of a stick through a stagnant pool of rain water. His own image was gone as well.

He crossed the hall. Chilled air streamed in through an open window. Chance pushed the heavy glass door open and stepped out into the garden. Taut branches laden with fresh shoots, slender stems with tiny sprouting buds shot upward. The garden lay calm, still sunk in repose. Wisps of clouds floated by and left the moon polished. Now and then, boughs rustled and gently shook off their drops of water. A breeze fell upon the foliage and nestled under the cover of its moist leaves. Not a thought lifted itself from Chance's brain. Peace filled his chest.

Born on June 14, 1933, of Mieczyslaw and Elzbieta Kosinski in Lodz, Poland, Jerzy Kosinski came to the United States in 1957. He was naturalized in 1965. Mr. Kosinski obtained M.A. degrees in social sciences and history from the University of Lodz, and as a Ford Foundation Fellow completed his postgraduate studies in sociology at both the Polish Academy of Sciences in Warsaw and Columbia University in New York. He wrote *The Future Is Ours, Comrade* (1960) and *No Third Path* (1962), both collections of essays he published under the pen name of Joseph Novak. He is the author of the novels *The Painted Bird* (1965), *Steps* (1968), *Being There* (1971), *The Devil Tree* (first edition 1973, revised in 1981), *Cockpit* (1975), *Blind Date* (1977), *Passion Play* (1979), *Pinball* (1982), and *The Hermit of 69th Street* (1988).

As a Guggenheim Fellow, Mr. Kosinski studied at the Center for Advanced Studies at Wesleyan University; subsequently he taught American prose at Princeton and Yale universities. He then served the maximum two terms as president of the American Center of P.E.N., the international association of writers and editors. He was also a Fellow of Timothy Dwight College at Yale University. Mr. Kosinski founded and served as president of the Jewish Presence Foundation, based in New York.

Mr. Kosinski won the National Book Award for *Steps,* the American Academy of Arts and Letters Award in literature, best Screenplay of the Year Award for *Being There* from both the Writers Guild of America and the British Academy of Film and Television Arts (BAFTA), the B'rith Shalom Humanitarian Freedom Award, the Polonia Media Award, the American Civil Liberties Union First Amendment Award and International House Harry Edmonds Life Achievement Award. He was a recipient of honorary Ph.D.s in Hebrew letters from Spertus College of Judaica and in humane letters from both Albion College, Michigan (1988) and Potsdam College of New York State University (1989).

An adept of photographic art, with one-man exhibitions to his credit in Warsaw's State Crooked Circle Gallery (1957), André Zarre Gallery in New York (1988), and in the Spertus College of Judaica in Chicago (1992), Mr. Kosinski was also an avid polo player and skier. In his film-acting debut in Warren Beatty's *Reds,* he portrayed Grigori Zinoviev, the Russian revolutionary leader.

Mr. Kosinski died in New York on May 3, 1991.